# BLOOD BANK

## A CHARITABLE ANTHOLOGY

"Laws of Virulence" reprinted with permission–first appearance *Warmed and Bound: A Velvet Anthology*, 2011. "We Can Get Them for You Wholesale" reprinted with permission–first appearance *Knave*, 1984.

All other stories are original to this volume and are copyright © 2022 to their respective authors.

ISBN: 978-1-940250-53-3

This book is a work of fiction. Names, characters, business organizations, places, events and incidents either are the product of the authors' imaginations or are used fictitiously. Any resemblance to actual persons, living or dead, events or locales is entirely coincidental.

Cover art by Drew Stepek
www.Godless.com

Interior Layout by Lori Michelle
www.theauthorsalley.com

Printed in the United States of America

First Edition

Visit us on the web at:
www.bloodboundbooks.net

# SPREADING HOPE THROUGH DARK FICTION

*BLOOD BANK* IS more than just an anthology. It's a milestone for Blood Bound Books. A symbolic culmination in an evolutionary journey, I didn't realize we were on until recently.

A lot has changed since Joseph and I opened Blood Bound Books in 2009. Back then, a major goal of mine was to scare and shock people. To be totally indie and extreme, remembered for changing the world of horror fiction in ways only a non-conformist can.

I'd like to believe Blood Bound Books accomplished this. I'd also like to believe we've gotten better with age. The only thing I know for sure though, is that over the years I've become a different person and my goals have shifted. I still want to change the world, but I'm no longer concerned about it being the world of fiction.

More important than the legacy of 'best', 'scariest', or some other arbitrary title, I now want the company to be remembered for making a positive impact in the lives of children. So in 2019, Blood Bound Books changed its mission to: Spreading Hope Through Dark Fiction. I called *Blood Bank* a symbolic culmination because while it is not the end of this journey by any means, it is the biggest undertaking so far in this new trajectory—a five-year fundraiser for *Read Better Be Better* and *Hagar's House.*

I now understand those who write and publish dark fiction have a huge responsibility. Horror and its numerous subgenres are not simply mindless stories of blood and guts, depressing and revolting topics—though I assure you many tales in this anthology are bleak. Dark fiction reflects aspects of real life. Aspects that make us uncomfortable, that trigger us, yet these topics are realities for many people in the world. In this book, there may be stories you enjoy more than others, but each author had a reason for giving life to the tale they contributed. We can learn much about ourselves and others through a horror story. We can grow and evolve. Perhaps like me, you're on a journey of evolution and don't realize it yet. After all, humans can only know light by first observing the dark.

It is crucial that we, each one of us, strive to contain the horrors of real life to the pages of fiction. Let's explore the depths of our own shadows through fictional characters rather than against one another. And as we come to know ourselves through the reading of dark fiction, we can better cultivate the main character we want to emulate in our own lives.

My deepest thanks to the authors who donated to this project, all the producers listed in the acknowledgements for their financial support, Drew Stepek & Godless for the cover art, and of course, you. Your purchase of this anthology has improved childhood literacy in Arizona and is giving displaced families in New Orleans a bit of peace during their own horrors.

Spreading hope through dark fiction is not what birthed Blood Bound Books, but it *is* our future. In addition to *Blood Bank*, we are still giving away free books for blood donations, stocking classrooms with much needed literature, and supporting Shriner's Hospitals.

If you'd like to know more, please visit us online at www.BloodBoundBooks.com

Thanks again,

Marc Ciccarone/S.C. Mendes

Dear Reader,

Thank you for purchasing this anthology and supporting Read Better Be Better (RBBB). Our organization was founded in 2014 to fight Arizona's ongoing literacy crisis. Students that aren't reading at grade level by the end of third grade are four times less likely to graduate from high school, but with proper intervention—students who are reading at grade level or higher have an 89 percent chance of graduating regardless of their socioeconomic status.

RBBB firmly believes that literacy can change lives and our mission is to connect young readers and youth leaders to inspire a love of literacy and learning. Our after-school program serves second to fourth-grade "Readers" who have been identified by their teachers as needing targeted reading intervention. The Readers are paired for a semester with middle to high school "Leaders" who have volunteered for the program.

Through twice-weekly sessions lasting 90 minutes each, RBBB seeks to improve Readers' concentration, understanding, and confidence, as well as the Leaders' responsibility, accountability, and confidence. RBBB's training for Leaders emphasizes the importance of their role in bolstering their Reader's growth and empowering them as changemakers and advocates for their communities. Both Leaders and Readers are instilled with RBBB's values of being Excellent and Kind through their work and interactions with each other, Program Coaches, and their communities.

With the implementation of our evidence-based program, Readers improve 16 percent more than nonparticipating students on standardized reading comprehension tests. To date, 88 percent of Readers report that they "understand what they are reading more than they did before participating in RBBB". Additionally, 87 percent of Leaders report they now "have what it takes to be a good leader" after participating.

Now more than ever, Arizona students need our help. The COVID-19 crisis has only widened the educational divide in our state, especially in reading comprehension. Your purchase of this book helps us reach students that need us most and give them the tools they need to be successful both now and in the future. We are so thankful for your support.

With gratitude,

Sophie Allen-Etchart
CEO & Founder of Read Better Be Better
sophie@readbetterbebetter.org
www.readbetterbebetter.org

Friends,

Thank you so much for supporting Hagar's House through your purchase and reading of this book.

Hagar's House (www.HagarsHouseNola.org) serves as a sanctuary for women, children and gender non-conforming folks in New Orleans. Our home provides an open and compassionate residential community, resource coordination and a safe space to transition into permanent housing by offering:

- A beautiful, clean, safe place to rest and call home
- An open and empowering space that welcomes women, children and gender non-conforming folks
- An intentional community that is actively engaged in undoing the root causes of poverty
- Holistic programming focused on physical health, emotional/spiritual health and social justice
- A Capacity Building partnership where residents meet weekly with staff to set their own long and short-term goals and to determine their own path for meeting those goals
- A savings program in which working residents save 70% of their income, ideally $3,000 at the time of moving out
- Healthy food and space to plant in a community garden

Hagar's House is a program of the 501(c)(3) nonprofit First Grace Community Alliance (FGCA). The mission of FGCA is to work with and for people in need, especially women and their children, by meeting food, housing and other emergency needs, while simultaneously challenging systemic poverty in the greater New Orleans area. FGCA does this through its two programs: 1) Hagar's House and 2) Project Ishmael, our children's immigration legal program (www.ProjectIshmaelNola.org) that provides free legal representation to local children at risk of deportation.

Again, thank you for being in this work with us through this book.

In peace and gratitude,

Angela Davis
Co-founder and Executive Director

# TABLE OF CONTENTS

# CLOWN DOLL

JO KAPLAN

CHARLENE WOKE IN the middle of the night to the sound of manic laughter.

First, she checked the time—3:17 a.m. by the digital green numbers that cut through the dark at her bedside—and then, blinking away sleep, she felt for her boyfriend who had become a warm lump of blankets beside her.

"Karl," she murmured, gently shoving his shoulder.

The laughter came and went in peals, like a wave. It was coming from outside.

They lived in a one-bedroom apartment nestled in a courtyard building on one of those narrow hilly streets in Los Angeles. Their place was on the second floor, shadowed by the looming behemoth of a cemetery, one of its rolling hills crowned by a massive white cross. The living room window offered a generous view of the carport below. From the bedroom, you could see the courtyard, where a fountain burbled.

Since it was never fully dark in Los Angeles, the reddish haze of city light permeated the window. Its missing slats where cheap blinds had fallen out gave it a gap-toothed grin. Charlene rolled out of bed and crept to the window to peer out of one empty spot that let in a vague line of semi-darkness. The courtyard lights never went out, so she could see the grassy area below illuminated by a dull yellow glow.

There, she spotted the culprit.

It was two weeks until Halloween, and their neighbor, Dan—an aging pothead who frequently worked on his pickup in the carport while blasting classic rock—had decorated the entrance to his apartment in the courtyard below. Fake spiderwebs clung to the shrubs, and an ugly clown puppet dangled on a string, one of those annoying props with a motion sensor that gives its hideous laugh any time someone walks past.

But no one was walking past at three o'clock in the morning.

Instead, a woman stood in front of the dangling puppet, her arms reaching up to clutch it in both hands. She shook the toy, and the puppet laughed and laughed and laughed.

"What the fuck?" Karl muttered, finally rousing.

"It's Dan's wife," said Charlene as she stepped aside to let her boyfriend peer out the window.

"What the hell is she doing?"

"Maybe she's trying to take it down?"

Karl squinted through the gap in the blinds. "Maybe it's broken and she's trying to fix it."

"By shaking it?"

Karl shrugged. "If she keeps it up, I'll go down there."

"I'm sure she'll stop," said Charlene, not sure at all.

"You want to listen to that all night?"

Of course she didn't, but neither did she relish the idea of Karl confronting a hostile stranger in the courtyard—not that Dan's wife would be hostile, but they really didn't know her, and only knew Dan as the easy-going middle-aged guy who sometimes signed for their packages when they weren't home. Karl's scarecrow-like frame made it nearly impossible to imagine him intimidating anyone. The problem was he *thought* he could be intimidating, and that's what really worried Charlene. Like the time that bearded hipster guy had started smoking cigarettes right outside of their window, the smell permeating into their apartment at eight o'clock in the morning, and he had finally gone down to tell him to smoke somewhere else. She had watched from above, looking down on their heads in the carport. The guy was twice as big as Karl and for a moment seemed about to tell him to fuck off, based on the dark brewing in his eyes and the way he kept blowing smoke in Karl's face. Charlene had felt the moment of tension in her bones, as if she were down there herself—she hated the way she internalized the anxiety of the world around her—but at last, the guy had shrugged and walked away.

"Someone else will have woken up," she reasoned as they stood huddled against the window. "Don't you think? Arman will hear, and he'll go tell her to be quiet."

Arman, the apartment manager, was a chummy, balding man who, in spite of his general good humor, never hesitated to chastise the kids who ran amok in the carport, or to tell off inconsiderate motorists who blocked the driveway.

"I don't see any lights on in his apartment."

"We can't be the only ones hearing this."

Karl rolled his eyes. "Maybe everyone else is doing the same thing we are, waiting for someone else to go take care of it."

"She isn't *crazy*, is she? I mean, she doesn't have some kind of . . . mental issue?"

"Hell, how would I know?"

"Or maybe it's some kind of Halloween prank?"

"I don't give a shit *why* she's doing it," said Karl. "I just want her to stop so I can fucking sleep."

The night, the unforgiving reddish haze of the city, and the starkness of the courtyard lights conspired to make the sound of laughter impel a strange disturbance into the air like ripples in the ocean, soundwaves in a thick polluted night lapping against her brain.

They were no strangers to unusual sounds in the night. Not here, in L.A. Sirens blared, helicopters went waffling overhead; once, bloodcurdling screams had shaken them at midnight. They never found out who it was. They decided it must be an actor rehearsing for an audition. None of their business. And then there was the obscene growl of the G-Class that went in and out of the carport at two in the morning, the blaring of Armenian dance music, the crying of neighbor children up far past their bedtime, the eerie howl of coyotes in the surrounding hills.

All manner of sounds made the city a peculiar place. But none, somehow, disturbed Charlene more than the pre-recorded laughter of the clown puppet. It crept up and down the crevices of her spine.

"That's it," said Karl. "I'm going out there."

Her heart lurched. She felt afraid for him, as if it would be *her* going out there to confront the woman. Like the way she always pressed an imaginary brake when sitting in the passenger's seat of Karl's car, unable to close her eyes and allow him to guide them down the road. Until he came back up to the apartment, she would feel every bit of tension, as if she were the one out there. Even observing the world was too much, sometimes. She was like a sponge left out in the rain, absorbing every stabbing drop.

"Wait another minute, in case someone else is heading out to talk to her. Let them deal with it."

Karl made a sound in the back of his throat. Charlene wished she could be easygoing, carefree. Not riddled with every feeling the city threw at her with its deafening traffic, the groaning footsteps every time someone passed on the walkway outside their apartment, the noise of neighbors whose communication style seemed to be composed solely of shouting. It made her want to curl up in a ball and cocoon herself, her and Karl, and pretend they weren't part of it.

"I don't see anyone else going out there," he said and started pulling on his shoes. He took a moment to peer out the peephole—a habit he had probably picked up from Charlene, who always wanted to be sure she wouldn't accidentally open the door with anyone nearby—and opened the front door onto the deserted walkway.

It was darker there, covered, looking across to the little alcove where the neighbors left a ratty computer chair by their own door. Karl stepped out, and Charlene listened to his footsteps groan across the walkway, which ran along their windowless wall. Following the sound, she went back to the bedroom to peer out the window.

The woman was still shaking the puppet.

What a terrible sound was laughter, Charlene thought. When it went on and on, with nothing funny happening—when it simply continued. It was madness.

She spotted Karl heading down the staircase and watched him cross the dewy grass. He spoke to the woman. Charlene did not hear what he said. She considered opening the window but decided against it, fearing that if she heard the conversation, it would put her even more *down there* with them, when she just wanted to be here, safe in her little apartment.

People frightened her because she didn't know what lurked inside of them. If it was the same sort of storm that lived in her. And this woman, in particular, seemed inscrutable, unpredictable.

Karl came up beside the woman, and her girth obscured him from Charlene's view. Perhaps he was asking her what she was doing.

Charlene nearly shouted with relief when the woman finally let go of the clown and stepped away from it. At merciful last, its laughter subsided. The quiet held a note of expectant calm.

The woman turned and crossed the courtyard. Charlene expected to see Karl turn to her and give her a thumbs up, but he remained where he stood, looking up at the dangling puppet, perhaps trying to determine what the woman had been trying to do with it.

Then he reached up and took hold of it. Charlene thought he might be looking for an off switch or trying to take it down. He gave it a little shake, and the laughter burbled up again. Charlene winced. It must have been an accident.

But then he shook it again.

She wanted to slam her fist against the window. Was this some sort of joke?

Her attention skittered when she noticed a figure emerging from the stairwell. The woman had come up to the second floor instead of returning to her own apartment. She walked with a slow, uneven gait, as if taking great pains to control all of her limbs—just a large, lumbering shadow dragging itself across the walkway.

As the woman came closer, Karl continued shaking the clown in the courtyard. It laughed and laughed. But it wasn't genuine, was it? It was the laughter of the demented, laughter devoid of humor or mirth. Laughter for its own sick sake.

Why are you laughing? She wanted to scream. What is there to laugh about?

Suddenly the woman's face appeared in the window.

Charlene lurched backward.

Through the thin veneer of glass, her face loomed like a full moon in the semi-darkness. A pair of blank, dead eyes stared through the window, and below those oddly lifeless eyes stretched a vast, ear-to-ear grin.

Charlene cursed the cheap blinds that fell down even after Arman replaced them. She worried about someone peeking through the empty slats. Here was a pale fleshy face pressed against the glass, and she could not even pull the blinds to block it out.

There was no mirth in the grin. It stretched her face grotesquely. Lines of blood split the middle of the strained lips. Slightly crooked teeth lined up like tombstones in the mouth's darkness.

At last, the woman peeled herself from the window and began stumping away. Below, Karl continued to shake the puppet, eliciting its laughter. Only now he had turned his face up toward their bedroom window. Grinning.

And as the woman's footfalls moved away, she realized where they were going—around the corner, down the walkway outside her windowless hall.

Toward the front door.

Feet flew her through the apartment, and she twisted the lock before those footfalls could make it there.

When they did, the doorknob twisted one way and then the other, giving a little rattle. Charlene backed up, heart pounding. Why was this woman trying to get into her apartment? Was she lost? Confused? What was *wrong* with her?

The doorknob stopped rattling.

Charlene pressed her eye to the peephole.

A dark shape occupied the neighbor's chair. It was large, fleshy.

The lights did not quite reach the shadow. It was like the figures she used to think she saw as a child, in her bedroom at night—all manner of shapes that could be anything, that might rear up to attack her when she closed her eyes.

She pulled back, and that's when she heard the slow, heavy footfalls coming down the walkway. Groaning, step by step, along the windowless wall. Someone stopped on the other side of the door. Charlene's heart stood in her throat. The doorknob rattled.

A fist banged.

"Karl? Is that you?"

No answer. She knew it *must* be him. Why wouldn't he answer?

Trembling hands found her phone, but she was at a loss for who to call. The police? No one had committed a crime.

And now she could hear that old voice in her head, the one at parties that told her no one wanted to hear about homeless women raped on Skid Row, or the impending existential crisis of wildfire season; everyone just wants to have a good time. Shut up and stop being such a worrywart, Charlene. Stop being so negative, so anxious, so concerned. Just relax and have fun. Be yourself. Smile. Laugh, once in a while.

That voice often sounded like Karl. After all, he'd told her all those things, at some point or other, in the course of their relationship.

She was simply too full of everything except for herself. Sometimes she drank just to empty her *self* out of herself.

She found Arman's number in her phone. She hit "call." The phone rang in her ear once, twice. Again.

No answer.

When his voicemail picked up, she angrily thumbed the "end call" button and scrolled through her contacts. She remembered the time she and Karl had gone out of town for a wedding and had asked Dan to water their plants. She had saved his number.

She found it.

The phone rang.

"Huh—hello?" a groggy voice emerged from the other end of the line.

There was relief, of a kind. But she hesitated, wordless.

"Carlos? Jesus Christ, the answer is no, I'm not picking you up again, I don't care where you woke up this time—"

"No," she cut in. "No, it's Charlene, from apartment 23."

Dan grunted. "Charlene? What the . . . Jesus Christ, why are you calling me at . . . three-thirty in the morning?"

"I'm sorry. But—there's something weird going on outside your apartment."

She sensed him growing alert on the other end. Rustling, movement—maybe drawing back a curtain to peer out the window. "What is it? What's going on?"

"A few minutes ago, your wife was outside—"

"My wife?" he cut in. There was a pause. "My wife is here in bed. Dead asleep."

The back of Charlene's neck prickled.

Who was the figure sitting in the neighbor's chair?

"Then . . . then *someone* was outside your apartment, messing with your Halloween decorations. You know, the one that laughs?"

"Huh?"

"The clown. The one that laughs when you walk past."

"No," said Dan. "No, I'm pretty sure we don't have a clown decoration. Christ, I hate those things. Can't stand motion-sensors, either."

Charlene sputtered. "But . . . "

"Look, why are you calling? Is everything okay?"

"I don't . . . " She glanced back to the front door where she knew Karl was still standing. Waiting. "I don't know. I locked Karl out."

"Why did you do that?"

She shook her head. "I don't know. He seemed . . . different."

"Well, why don't you let him in?"

Dan's voice had changed subtly. Its cadence. It was like a flat line. Charlene's breath caught in her throat, and her voice came out a whisper. "What?"

"Why . . . " said Dan, his voice crackling, shifting, in her ear, "don't . . . you . . . let . . . him . . . "

A bang on the front door.

" . . . IN?"

With a gasp, Charlene dropped her phone, which erupted in crackling peals of laughter, like electric lights popping. She saw the call had been disconnected—and that it had only lasted fifteen seconds. But that wasn't right. They'd spoken for at least a minute.

Another bang on the door.

"Karl?" she said again, trying to raise her voice above a shaky murmur. Hesitantly, she approached the door, leaned in, looked out the peephole.

Darkness.

She blinked, hoping to adjust her eyes after staring at the brightness of her phone. How many times had she hesitated here, waiting for the neighbor across the way to get up from the chair and go back inside? She perceived that shape still sitting in the chair in the dark.

It was too much, sometimes, being around people. She internalized every moment of awkwardness and embarrassment that she found lurking in the corners of the world. She was the shy girl at the coffeeshop trying to strike up a conversation with the attractive barista. She was the idiot who got lost while driving in a new neighborhood and could never decide which street to turn down. She was the student who had been called on and found his mind horrifically blank. This insecurity had plagued her all her life. She'd thought living with Karl might make her more sure of things, but it hadn't. The only one to guide her was herself, and sometimes she wasn't confident she had any business being behind the wheel of her own life.

She didn't know what to do.

The figure in the chair stood up.

She only had to wait until the person left, and then she would run down to the carport, get in her car, and . . . get the hell away from here. Go somewhere. She didn't know where. Maybe to her parents' house. It was only a forty-minute drive.

The figure took a step away from the chair, out of the shadows that crawled in that alcove, and into the dull light that permeated the walkway. Now free to look without fear of being seen, Charlene observed the woman and realized she wore a pair of ratty pajamas, dirty and frayed, red with white polka dots. She was barefoot, the tops of her feet fish-belly white.

The woman opened and shut her mouth, as if trying to speak, but nothing emerged from the creak of her jaws behind those stretched-out lips.

The lights of the building flickered—not like an electrical fluctuation, but more like when a large shape, a cloud, moves over the moon.

The woman began to shake.

At first, Charlene thought it was a seizure. But as her limbs flailed and her body jerked left and right, it looked more as if she were *being shaken* by something. Eyes rolled up white in her head. A burble of laughter emerged from her lips, echoing in the alcove behind her. She laughed and laughed.

Charlene grabbed her keys and went back to the bedroom, pushed the blinds to the side. Two more dislodged and clattered to the floor. She slid open the sticky old window, pried up the edges of the screen, and popped it free. But as she climbed onto the sill to jump down to the walkway below, she looked out, hoping to spot Karl.

She didn't see him.

She didn't see the clown puppet, either.

Where it had been suspended on its string, there was nothing.

Her skin prickled. She thought it most likely that Karl had taken it down, yet part of her could not help but imagine that all that shaking had finally pulled loose the string from which it dangled, setting it free—to skitter off on hollow legs; to crouch in the darkness like a spider.

Charlene dropped onto the walkway and padded for the staircase that led down to the courtyard, at the other end of which there was an archway underneath the second-floor apartments leading to the carport, where her trusty old Nissan with the dinged-up bumper waited. She could still hear the woman's laughter as she descended the stairs, and she thought there was more than just the woman's voice in it. Yet it sounded automatic, repetitive, as if recorded and looped.

Charlene's bare feet met the cool, dewy grass of the courtyard. On all four sides, two stories of apartments rose up around her, and she wondered if the people inside were so deeply asleep they hadn't heard a thing. Or if they were dangling from doorways, unable to get down.

She made it to the other side of the courtyard and entered the dark tunnel that led to the carport. From the lights on the other side, she could see a silhouette hanging from the end of the passageway.

Karl.

Karl hanged on a string.

Karl dangling, still but for the gentle creak from side to side as the wind prodded him.

Karl grinning, dripping blood, eyes rolled up white, empty grin revealing the emptiness inside his hollowed-out form.

Karl's bones clanking like a wooden wind chime.

Charlene dropped her keys.

She bent down, staring at the ground, not at the figure hanging on the other end of the passage, searching for her keys, running her hands through the darkness until her fingers found the metal. Snatching them, she stood up again—she had to look—

She blinked. Stepped closer.

It was not Karl.

It was the clown puppet.

It hung there at the end of the passage, blocking her way.

She considered turning back, but she didn't know where the woman was, if she was still in front of her apartment. If she was blocking the front entrance now. She couldn't hear her laughing anymore.

All she needed to do was sidle around the puppet, and she would be free.

Charlene stepped closer, seeing more of its detail. Its white cue ball eyes, pupils having long ago worn off, stared blankly into her above its empty grin. Everything about it was worn, old. Its red polka-dot clothing and painted mouth had faded to a dingy color like dried blood.

The more she gazed at it, the more she recognized something of its hollowness. She felt her mouth stretching wide with something that was not quite amusement.

The light behind the puppet flickered again, like something behemoth passing over it, something pulling on its strings, and Charlene felt the invisible hand reach up to take hold of her. Then she understood what was so funny. That nothing was funny. That nothingness could be so funny. She felt her bones rattle like hollow wooden legs, and she started to laugh, wondering what would happen when she was finally shaken free of her strings.

# FOOL'S BLOOD

RENA MASON

HOT STINKING BREATHS gusted Billy's chilled skin as he stared up at the stars in front of his newly purchased mine in Elko, Nevada. Billy glanced at the dark hole that reminded him of a man screaming through a broken jaw, but that didn't quell his excitement for staking out a claim in his name. He owned something now, a piece of land he could pass down to a new generation of Hills. The thought tingled the base of his neck as if mice scurried around it. He only wished his pa were alive to see it all.

*'Go west'* were William Hill Senior's last words as he passed on cradled in Billy's arms, unable to fight off the sickness that came with taking a bluebelly bayonet through his gut. Being the last two Hills from Jackson Parish, Billy thanked the Lord he and his pa got to serve together in the Twelfth. All three of Billy's brothers would've been jealous had any of them survived. Their pa was one of the best Jackson Sharpshooters in Buford's Brigade.

It had taken him three years to settle his family's affairs and gather up the money after the war, but Billy wanted nothing more than to up and leave home. Life in the South had changed, and as eager as the prospects had made him when his pa was alive, his pa's *'West'* wasn't anything like either one of them had imagined and talked about.

A low moan resonated from the dark mouth in the rockface and rattled Billy's chest.

"Just the wind," he said, knowing full well no wind he'd ever heard before made that sound. But since he'd got to Elko and its endless desert of rocks, dirt, and bramble, strange noises came in abundance.

Unable to sleep under the bright light of the moon, he sat up and shook his sleeves, and then gently swiped at them with the backs of his hands. Scorpions dropped to the ground. Wary, their stingers up, they took their time moving away. Billy pricked his ears and listened for the slow rattle of a snake. He knew better than to make any sudden movements. Three weeks' time was all it took him to learn the most important things. Well, that and the townsfolk were plenty eager to give Billy advice on just about everything. Mighty helpful while he handed over his money. Not so much when he'd got low. It was up to him now to get to work mining. If he made money, they made money. They'd be friendly again. He learned that quick too. His pa would be proud of how smart he'd gotten.

He stood and stretched, hesitant about crawling through the low, cramped entrance to begin digging. For the second time in his life, he was thankful to be thin and small. The first and last time he'd gone inside was before he bought it. About twenty feet in, one shaft forked into two. 'Delgado digs 'em tight as a coffin,' the supply store owner had said. Billy had half-listened to the chatter while buying supplies in town, keeping his eyes on the trade man's daughter, Melinda. Billy wanted to marry her and have a new family of Hills after he struck it rich.

He shuddered thinking of the stench that rose up the shafts, belching their damp earth and metal stink, so much like the smell of blood. Billy knew that particular odor well. During the war, he'd crawled his way through mounds of piled bodies made up of Confederate and Union soldiers. He noticed no difference between the dying men. All of them bled the same, stunk the same, some still alive and moaning, eyes open and staring right through him. He had feared for his life, being buried alive under 'em. But those were tough days, and he felt no shame in it. That fear is what had kept him moving, kept him alive. And so, he'd do it again, scrabble his way to the gold, and for glory this time.

Billy shook off the chill as he finished relieving himself. A coyote laughed from afar. Billy straightened out his drawers and then kicked a rock in the direction of the yip-howls. He hated the damn animals and couldn't help but take their cackling as jeers against him.

He thought about the man who'd dug out the shafts before him. The deeds clerk had said Señor Delgado had done it all by himself. A Spaniard, he'd said. Struck a decent chunk of gold that had made him rich enough to register another claim for a bigger piece of outlying land about fifty miles northwest, Tusca-something. No longer in need, the Spaniard had sold off all his smaller claims around Elko, and Billy had bought the one where the man's gold had come from. A part of him couldn't help but wonder if the deeds clerk told tall tales just to sell worthless mines.

Voices echoed up and out of the mine. A clinking noise came next. He'd gotten used to the voices, or whatever it was that sounded like people talking, the moaning, howling, crying, and plenty of other sounds, but he'd not heard clinking before. He considered lighting a lamp but didn't want to waste the kerosene.

"Someone in there?" He stepped back and shouted down into the dark mouth.

It quieted, which wasn't right neither. The mine had never been quiet, particularly at night. Then footsteps came, boots thumping like a heartbeat and growing louder. Billy moved further away, scanned the ground for his shovel. He crouched down and grabbed it, giving the handle a shake to let off any scorpions.

At the cave entrance, nimble shadows felt their way around the mouth like feelers and then became hands and fingers. Billy walked toward the rockface and readied his shovel to strike.

"You better make yourself known right quick," he said.

A human figure dragged and pulled itself out and then stood at arms' length, towering over Billy by at least a foot, maybe more.

"Answer me, stranger." Billy turned the sharp edge of the shovel and leaned in. He wanted to touch the dark figure with it. Why could he see everything else in the moon's light except for this man?

"Get that out of my face, boy," a deep voice said.

"So, you are real," Billy whispered to himself. Then he said aloud, "Not until you tell me who you are, and what you're doing in *my* mine."

The man roared, more mocking than the coyote's laughter.

"Dammit! Stop—" Billy dropped the shovel and launched himself forward. He slammed into the man as if he'd hit a wall. The tall stranger didn't waver, and Billy clung to him like a child jumping and wanting to be picked up and carried. Billy slid down until his feet touched the ground and then he reached for the shovel again.

White light and pain exploded from the side of his head and then he saw nothing else.

Billy's breathing grew heavy and labored. As soon as the train had crossed the state line, he felt the last drop of Louisiana moisture evaporate from his body. This desert heat burned and stung as if he stood next to a crackling wildfire. He tried to keep any bare skin out of the searing sunlight. It hurt. Every hour or so, he'd rise and stand near an open window or door to let his sweaty clothes dry. He swore in the few minutes it took he was freezing to death. He couldn't be right about that though and figured the heat had gotten to his head.

Finally out onto the platform, he could almost taste gold in the air. Then a brown swirl of dirt spun around him, leaving him with nothing but the earthy tang and crunch of dirt in his mouth.

*Welcome to Elko.*

Town consisted of a main street that bisected two long rows of one-story wood buildings. He noted a bank, a hotel, a supply store, and other small establishments out to make their share from prospectors and travelers passing through. Behind the wood buildings stood a bunch of shanties and tents, and beyond that, dry desert land and red clay mountains that went on forever.

A moist breeze, heady with foreign aromas came up behind him. Billy spun around and found himself in a mirage. High white walls inlaid with beautiful colored tiles made up floral patterns and shapes that surrounded him on all sides. Magnificent architecture like he'd never seen before towered above. He lowered his eyes, squeezed them shut, and then rubbed them with his fingers to clear out any dirt.

Rectangular pools with flowing green water and fountains filled his path. He walked toward one and drank his fill, taking everything in. *Had he died on the train?*

A man in robes, his head swathed in fabric, walked past the entryway of a building just ahead. Billy rushed after him and entered a circular room with ceilings of stone. He stopped and held his breath as his eyes looked up and saw artfully carved stalactites set like honeycomb in shapes of stars, painted a blue like the night sky. The walls and pillars also had inlaid tiles in floral shapes more beautiful than real flowers. So many brilliant colors and patterns. The robed man stood in front of smooth tiles with foreign writing, but somehow Billy understood it.

*"Be sparse in words and you will go in peace."*

He intended to do just that. Billy stepped next to the man and nodded. The man smiled and put his palm against Billy's back, guiding him to another room.

Massive wood tables, every inch covered in tall glass shapes, steam and smoke rising from them, jars filled with dust, rocks, dried flowers, and plants, took up all the space. More rooms of the same went on and on in a circle around the inside of the building. Men worked at these tables, writing in books, reading from them, talking among themselves. Soft, melodic music drifted through the windows along with that soft, moist breeze, ruffling vibrant fabrics as thin as the air itself. Their deep shades hung in wide ribbons from the walls.

The robed man asked Billy a question, but Billy couldn't think of how to respond. The man shook Billy's shoulder. Then again, but harder, almost hurting him.

"Stop that," Billy said.

"Son, it's time you woke—"

"Pa?" Billy opened his eyes, certain he'd died and gone to Heaven, or someplace else.

A man stood in front of him. One he thought he remembered. Then the star on the man's shirt brought his sense back.

"Sheriff? What're you—" Billy sat up.

"Take it easy, son," the sheriff said. "Señor Delgado here says your head hit a rock pretty hard when you tripped and fell."

"I, I didn't . . . Where am I?"

"My mine, boy." Señor Delgado stepped next to the sheriff. Both men hunched over Billy, eyeing him like captured prey.

Billy didn't retreat under their cold stares. He returned them, and got a good look at Delgado. The man's skin had tanned a deep shade of brown, but it didn't have the leathery, worn appearance of someone who'd labored under a burning sun. His thick, black, curly hair hung over his forehead, making his dark eyes more sinister than the man might've wanted. Billy knew plenty of folk whose families came from Spain and had settled in Louisiana, yet this foreigner had not one similar feature. Even his moustache and beard appeared wrong—too thick and dark.

Delgado quickly tucked his hair back up into the sweat-soaked scarf he'd wrapped around his head. The fabric seemed familiar, but Billy couldn't remember where he'd seen it before.

"What?" Billy said. "We were at *my* mine. That's right. You were in my mine, and then . . . "

"Then what?" Delgado said.

Billy didn't think it wise to mention that he'd attacked the man in front of the sheriff.

"I must've blacked out," Billy said. "Thing is, how did I get to your mine? I've no horse, just an ass, and you're nearly fifty miles out."

The sheriff rubbed his chin as if he hadn't thought of those particulars.

Delgado saw this and then quickly said, "I told you sheriff. He was walking around bewildered when I found him. Give him some time to rest here. I'll take him back to his mine when he's better."

The men stood and walked away from Billy. Delgado put his hand on the sheriff's back, guiding him out. The gesture recalled a familiarity in Billy's mind.

"Maybe I can convince him there's nothing for him here," Delgado said. "That he'd be better off back where he came from." He whispered the last part as if Billy wasn't right there.

The sheriff halted mid-stoop through a carved rock doorway and looked back. "You remember what happened, come and talk to me, son. A few of the folks in town are worried 'bout you."

"Yes, sir," Billy said. He hoped only for Melinda's concern.

The sheriff and Delgado left together, and Billy listened to them talking, their voices carried far through the air and across rock. Billy wondered at the size of Delgado's mine. *How could one Spaniard have done all this in such a short amount of time?* He sat up and thought his head might blow off. After composing himself, he moved slower, then rose, using the walls to keep steady. He walked over and picked up a lantern.

Billy ducked through the opening and glanced around. He headed the opposite way the men had gone.

A youthful voice, the kind that could've come from a boy or a girl, cried out ahead. Another narrow shaft opened up to his right. He raised the light, and a blast of hot air blew his hair back. Lucky for him, the lamp stayed lit. Billy stepped in, listening for the wailing. The supply store owner was right, the tunnel was tight as a coffin. Sharp edges plowed through his arms, and then the lamp went out. Heated gusts like the one that nearly baked his face on the way in traveled through the shafts and made high-pitched cries as they moved through the mine. That must've been the sound he'd heard before, not a child crying. Shoulder to shoulder against solid rock, Billy had to keep moving forward to find a space big enough to turn around. If he had this much trouble, no way Delgado could get through.

Stepping ahead and ever downward, Billy made his way to a larger, open area. He tripped over another lamp; the glass clinked but didn't break. He crouched down and pawed through the dirt floor for matches. Staying low, he found some, struck one on the wall and re-lit his lantern. Stacked wood crates came to light. Next to them, sat a couple of cots just off the floor, and another lamp. His flame flickered against hand-chiseled stone walls, setting fractured crystals in the rock alight, sparkling in the half-dark.

Glass jars and tubes, some of them broken, crowded the wall adjacent to the crates. He moved toward them. Delgado must be doing something down here other than mining. They reminded him of that mirage, but Billy couldn't recall exactly what the men did in all those rooms. He looked around for anything resembling a book or a notebook.

Billy bent over and put his nose to a large jar full of clear liquid. It had no odor. Curious, he stuck his finger into the liquid and then tasted it. Water. Billy tilted his head back and emptied the jar. He hadn't realized his thirst. A similar jar, still full, caught his eye. Billy replaced the one he'd drank from with it. He didn't think the Spaniard would take too kindly to his snooping.

Not finding any books, he headed back the way he came.

Nearing the entrance where he'd been left to rest, Billy's vision circled, his gut tingled, and he prayed the water he'd drank was just that and that it hadn't spoiled in some way or was tainted. It tasted good enough. Billy couldn't remember ever having a better drink of water. A scene of Melinda and him dancing at their wedding moved across the mine's ceiling.

His happy vision disappeared, broken up by more strange sounds. He hadn't seen any running water, but trickling, and rhythmic drips filled his ears. They sounded like a heart beating. The hot wind rushing through the shafts its breaths. Delgado's mines lived, and Billy yearned to find their hearts of gold.

"Follow me down, boy." Delgado's voice blared over the hypnotic pulsing and nearly shot Billy out of his boots. "There's something you ought to see." He slapped Billy's back and shoved him forward.

A potent gold fever gripped Billy. Maybe the jarred water put him out of sorts. Billy had to know all the man's secrets, so he went along without a fuss, hoping to gather anything he could.

"How'd you dig all this out in so short a time?"

"This was once a volcanic tunnel where molten rock used to flow. I found it quite by accident, I assure you."

They passed the shaft where Billy had found the jars of water. The space tightened around them as they continued downward. The air became humid and cooled. Billy's breathing became shallow, his head light, but his curiosity got the better of him. His body seemed to change shape and squeeze itself through an opening. Then the walls widened into a cavern. Down below, a pool of crystal-clear water. Above, stalactites that varied in size, water dripping from their tips, a vivid blue, even in the dim light.

"It's an underground spring, my boy, and a hundred times more valuable than all the gold in this desert. See, for hundreds, maybe even thousands of years, the rain's been collecting down here. I boil it to be sure it won't cause any sickness."

Billy thought of the glass containers filled with water in the room he'd found.

"What happened to your hand, boy? Looks like you cut it."

Billy hadn't noticed but wasn't surprised. Broken fragments had littered the entire area he'd sneaked off to. Delgado had sharp eyes if he could see the small line of dried blood so deep in the dark of the mine.

"I don't know," Billy said. "I can't remember. Anyhow, it'll be fine."

"You won't be so tough if it gets infected. Then you'll be worthless to the both of us. Those hands need to be in good shape for mining, right Billy?"

Billy didn't understand. Most days he was quick-witted, but he couldn't think straight or fast enough.

Delgado forced Billy to lead the way back and up to the room where he'd seen the jars.

"You're a lot bigger than me, Señor. How're you getting through this?"

"Don't worry about me, boy. I know my way. Stop ahead. Once you enter the small room there, have a seat on one of the cots."

They crowded into the room, and Delgado looked around, scouring the ground for anything disturbed, Billy thought. The tall man walked over to his makeshift laboratory and then opened up a brown leather case with smaller glass bottles inside. He pulled the vials out one at a time and read each label. Sometimes he opened one, smelled it, and then poured a little of its contents into a bowl. A few minutes later, he turned and brought the concoction over along with a roll of fabric.

"I've got something to fix that hand. Let me see. It looks nearly healed, but this will keep it clean." Delgado dipped the fabric into a green liquid and then squeezed it onto the wound.

"Ouch." Billy jerked away.

"Not so tough now then?"

"Begging your pardon, sir, but I grew up in Jackson Parish, Louisiana with three older brothers, and served in the 12th Infantry Regiment. I'm as tough as they come."

"I've seen stronger soldiers march across the parapets of Alhambra Palace. Much smarter ones, than you. They all died."

"Is that where you're from, in Spain? This palace?"

"The Alhambra didn't always belong to Spain."

"To who then?"

"My people."

"And who are your people is what I'm asking?"

"They called us Moors, boy."

"I knew you weren't a Spaniard."

"For centuries we studied and experimented. We are learned men. The wisest. We discovered how to make gold, how to heal, how to live forever with the Elixir of Life. We succeeded in all these things, but we did not intend to share our knowledge with a world we thought unworthy. We disbanded, moved to all the corners of the world, always keeping our secrets with us."

"Make gold?" Billy said. "You take me for a fool, old man? Bet I'm a lot smarter than you think. Learned in other ways."

"It takes blood, boy. Spilling innocent blood. The less innocent, the less gold, but that is why I have yet to strike a mother lode. Only clumps here and there. More experiments must be done. The knowledge comes slower without my brothers working side by side, although we seek one another out when we can."

Billy scratched his hand. The cut was gone. "What in the—" Billy wished he had a revolver, or his hunting knife.

"Like I said, boy. I have the power to heal."

But even the Moor had said that the cut had already appeared to be healing. How? Delgado had only just put the salve on his hand. Maybe this elixir the Moor had spewed on about had other powers.

"Why are you telling me all this?"

"Because you're going to die and become my next bit of gold."

Billy laughed. He couldn't help it. His manner had changed. He'd become foolhardy.

"You've been down in the mines too long, Señor. Maybe there's something in the water you've been drinking from that old pool you found. No way it only takes an innocent man's blood to make gold."

"Well, you're right in that. It does require a little more."

Billy raised his brow. "Since I'm a dead man anyhow, it'd sure be kindly of you to tell."

"Words from a special text," Delgado said. "They must be spoken aloud. You will believe me when you see it happening before your very own eyes."

"All right then. When does this show begin?"

"Now if you'd like."

"Right here?"

Delgado pointed. "Go over there and stand against the wall."

Billy nodded, astonished at his own goading and submission to this nonsense. But he wanted the recipe for making gold, and he wouldn't stop until he got it. It seemed the same arrogance that affected Delgado had taken him over as well. He rose from the cot and headed for the wall near all the glass jars and then leaned his left shoulder against it.

"This spot work?"

"As you wish," Delgado said.

"Is it gonna hurt?"

"Yes. Very much. But I thank you for being such a willing subject. You're the first one that has ever been so obliging, so I hope you don't mind if I take notes."

"Not at all," Billy said. He couldn't believe the gumption of this man. The arrogance.

Billy watched Delgado light a small fire. He positioned a glass bowl half an arm's length above the flames, held in place by a metal contraption, and then he poured some of the jarred and tubed liquids and powders into it. Delgado slid a book from the bottom of the brown leather box in a hidden compartment Billy hadn't seen before.

Delgado raised his voice and spoke his people's language, not Spanish.

Billy's eyes grew heavy, and he swore at times he understood Delgado. The singsong words reminded him of the music drifting through the window in the mirage. Billy's left ear itched, became warm, then hot. The stone wall next to his head fell into itself. The rock became swirling liquid. Billy stepped to the right.

"Don't move," Delgado said. "It's happening."

"What? The rock melting? I assumed you wanted that to happen. Is that where the gold is made? How is it gonna kill me?"

"Stop talking. Soon, the mine will speak to you."

"How?"

"Quiet and listen! Put your ear closer to it."

Billy heard whispering coming from the vortex, so he leaned in with all the confidence of an immortal. "Don't be too disappointed if this doesn't work, Señor. Remember, I'm far from innocent. Like I said, I fought in the war. Killed a lot of men."

"That doesn't make you less innocent, boy. It makes you a soldier who followed orders."

Many voices from the wall spoke softly of what he'd done. Billy saw it again in his mind, re-living all the details. How he'd crawled through those piles of dead men and pilfered their belongings. Reaching into their pockets, he took timepieces, wedding bands, precious heirlooms, gifts from fathers, mothers, and wives. Hell, he'd even pulled gold teeth, and taken anything of worth. Some items he yanked from the clutches of men still alive and dying. Their mouths often attempted to form words that became gasps of their last breaths. By God, he took it all. Billy howled at the pain assailing his ear.

"What is happening?" Delgado rushed over and pointed at something. "I've never seen this dark color before."

Delgado shoved Billy to the side, tearing Billy's ear off, separating him from the molten rock with the sound of a wet kiss.

"Ow!" Billy palmed the side of his head, hot blood gushing down his fingers and past his wrist.

"Aha! You see," Delgado shouted. "This is your value." The Moor reached up and took a small, dirty yellow clump from the churning stone. "Not worth a fraction of my effort. All the time it took me to find, collect, and prepare the ingredients." Delgado spat on Billy's boot.

"Just my one ear made that little bit of gold, you evil bastard."

"No. You didn't see. It was changing, turning black. That has never happened before. You must be so wretched a man that your blood becomes something else."

Red hot anger shot from Billy's ankles straight through his scalp. He sprang at Delgado, wrapping his legs around the man's chest, pinning his arms.

"How are you able to fight me?" Delgado stumbled. They struggled.

"You bastard! That's my ear. My gold." Billy snatched the nugget from the man's hand.

"Answer me. What did you do? You can't be as strong as me." Delgado turned to the water jars lining the wall. "No! You drank the Elixir of Life."

The stone vortex slowed. Before it came to a stop, Billy forced Delgado to move toward it and then wrenched his legs, thrusting Delgado forward. He grabbed hold of Delgado's head and put the man's face into the fluid wall.

Delgado's cries were muffled by the cooling rock. His arms flailed, every part of him trembled, jerked about, and then went slack. Billy fell as Delgado's body dropped from the rock. Delgado's face and the front half of his head gone. A rough surface of char covered what remained. Billy got up on all fours, looked around, and then scrabbled toward a few empty jars.

"If an innocent man's blood makes gold. What will yours make, Señor?" He rifled through Delgado's tools and got to work.

It didn't take much to convince the Elko sheriff Delgado had disappeared after two days while Billy lay recuperating. He was thankful the Elixir of Life had grown his ear back in that time. Billy left Tuscacora and headed over a hundred and fifty miles south to Eureka where he purchased a claim at Ruby Hill.

A year later, he put everything he'd learned together with Delgado's blood into the molten vortex of rock he called forth. The stone's color became dove gray and then the darkest black Billy had ever seen swelled up and swirled with the lighter shade, but the two never became one. Grays of every shade branched out across the mine walls, ground, and ceiling in flashes of lightning.

"I should've known your blood would be a darkness," Billy said. "Same as mine."

William Hill Jr. had struck one of the largest and richest silver-lead ore finds in history. He got his wish and married Melinda from Elko a month later. At his wedding, the sheriff told Billy that a man had come looking for Delgado and upon not finding him, wanted to know what had happened to his brother. The sheriff had explained the events, and then the man had asked for Billy's whereabouts. When Billy asked the sheriff what the man had looked like, the sheriff said, "A Spaniard."

# WE CAN GET THEM FOR YOU WHOLESALE

NEIL GAIMAN

PETER PINTER HAD never heard of Aristippus of the Cyrenaics, a lesser-known follower of Socrates who maintained that the avoidance of trouble was the highest attainable good; however, he had lived his uneventful life according to this precept. In all respects except one (an inability to pass up a bargain, and which of us is entirely free from that?), he was a very moderate man. He did not go to extremes. His speech was proper and reserved; he rarely overate; he drank enough to be sociable and no more; he was far from rich and in no wise poor. He liked people and people liked him. Bearing all that in mind, would you expect to find him in a lowlife pub on the seamier side of London's East End, taking out what is colloquially known as a 'contract' on someone he hardly knew? You would not. You would not even expect to find him in the pub.

And until a certain Friday afternoon, you would have been right. But the love of a woman can do strange things to a man, even one so colorless as Peter Pinter, and the discovery that Miss Gwendolyn Thorpe, twenty-three years of age, of 9 Oaktree Terrace, Purley, was messing about (as the vulgar would put it) with a smooth young gentleman from the accounting department—*after*, mark you, she had consented to wear an engagement ring, composed of real ruby chips, nine- carat gold, and something that might well have been a diamond (£37.50) that it had taken Peter almost an entire lunch hour to choose—can do very strange things to a man indeed.

After he had made this shocking discovery, Peter spent a sleepless Friday night, tossing and turning with visions of Gwendolyn and Archie Gibbons (the Don Juan of the Clamages accounting department) dancing and swimming before his eyes—performing acts that even Peter, if he were pressed, would have to admit were most improbable. But the bile of jealousy had risen up within him, and by the morning Peter had resolved that his rival should be done away with.

Saturday morning was spent wondering how one contacted an

assassin, for, to the best of Peter's knowledge, none were employed by Clamages (the department store that employed all three of the members of our eternal triangle, and, incidentally, furnished the ring), and he was wary of asking anyone outright for fear of attracting attention to himself.

Thus it was that Saturday afternoon found him hunting through the Yellow Pages.

ASSASSINS, he found, was not between ASPHALT CONTRACTORS and ASSESSORS (QUANTITY); KILLERS was not between KENNELS and KINDERGARTENS; MURDERERS was not between MOWERS and MUSEUMS. PEST CONTROL looked promising; however closer investigation of the pest control advertisements showed them to be almost solely concerned with "rats, mice, fleas, cockroaches, rabbits, moles, and rats" (to quote from one that Peter felt was rather hard on rats) and not really what he had in mind. Even so, being of a careful nature, he dutifully inspected the entries in that category, and at the bottom of the second page, in small print, he found a firm that looked promising.

*'Complete discreet disposal of irksome and unwanted mammals, etc.'* went the entry, *'Ketch, Hare, Burke and Ketch. The Old Firm.'* It went on to give no address, but only a telephone number.

Peter dialed the number, surprising himself by so doing. His heart pounded in his chest, and he tried to look nonchalant. The telephone rang once, twice, three times. Peter was just starting to hope that it would not be answered and he could forget the whole thing when there was a click and a brisk young female voice said, "Ketch Hare Burke and Ketch. Can I help you?"

Carefully not giving his name, Peter said, "Er, how big—I mean, what size mammals do you go up to? To, uh, dispose of?"

"Well, that would all depend on what size sir requires.'

He plucked up all his courage. "A person?"

Her voice remained brisk and unruffled. "Of course, sir. Do you have a pen and paper handy? Good. Be at the Dirty Donkey pub, off Little Courtney Street, E3, tonight at eight o'clock. Carry a rolled-up copy of the *Financial Times*—that's the pink one, sir—and our operative will approach you there." Then she put down the phone.

Peter was elated. It had been far easier than he had imagined. He went down to the newsagent's and bought a copy of the *Financial Times*, found Little Courtney Street in his *A-Z of London*, and spent the rest of the afternoon watching football on the television and imagining the smooth young gentleman from accounting's funeral.

It took Peter a while to find the pub. Eventually he spotted the pub sign, which showed a donkey and was indeed remarkably dirty.

The Dirty Donkey was a small and more or less filthy pub, poorly lit, in which knots of unshaven people wearing dusty donkey jackets stood around eyeing each other suspiciously, eating crisps and drinking pints of Guinness, a drink that Peter had never cared for. Peter held his *Financial Times* under one arm as conspicuously as he could, but no one approached him, so he bought a half of shandy and retreated to a corner table. Unable to think of anything else to do while waiting, he tried to read the paper, but, lost and confused by a maze of grain futures and a rubber company that was selling something or other short (quite what the short somethings were he could not tell), he gave it up and stared at the door.

He had waited almost ten minutes when a small busy man hustled in, looked quickly around him, then came straight over to Peter's table and sat down.

He stuck out his hand. "Kemble. Burton Kemble of Ketch Hare Burke Ketch. I hear you have a job for us."

He didn't look like a killer. Peter said so.

"Oh, lor' bless us, no. I'm not actually a part of our workforce, sir. I'm in sales."

Peter nodded. That certainly made sense. "Can we—er—talk freely here?"

"Sure. Nobody's interested. Now then, how many people would you like disposed of?"

"Only one. His name's Archibald Gibbons and he works in Clamages accounting department. His address is . . . "

Kemble interrupted. "We can go into all that later, sir, if you don't mind. Let's just quickly go over the financial side. First of all, the contract will cost you five hundred pounds . . . "

Peter nodded. He could afford that and in fact had expected to have to pay a little more.

" . . . although there's always the special offer," Kemble concluded smoothly.

Peter's eyes shone. As I mentioned earlier, he loved a bargain and often bought things he had no imaginable use for in sales or on special offers. Apart from this one failing (one that so many of us share), he was a most moderate young man. "Special offer?"

"Two for the price of one, sir."

Mmm. Peter thought about it. That worked out at only £250 each, which couldn't be bad no matter how you looked at it. There was only one snag. "I'm afraid I don't *have* anyone else I want killed."

Kemble looked disappointed. "That's a pity, sir. For two we could probably have even knocked the price down to, well, say four hundred and fifty pounds for the both of them."

"Really?"

"Well, it gives our operatives something to do, sir. If you must know" —and here he dropped his voice—"there really isn't enough work in this particular line to keep them occupied. Not like the old days. Isn't there just *one* other person you'd like to see dead?" Peter pondered. He hated to pass up a bargain, but couldn't for the life of him think of anyone else. He liked people. Still, a bargain was a bargain . . .

"Look," said Peter. "Could I think about it and see you here tomorrow night?"

The salesman looked pleased. "Of course, sir," he said. "I'm sure you'll be able to think of someone."

The answer—the obvious answer—came to Peter as he was drifting off to sleep that night. He sat straight up in bed, fumbled the bedside light on, and wrote a name down on the back of an envelope, in case he forgot it. To tell the truth, he didn't think that he could forget it, for it was painfully obvious, but you can never tell with these late-night thoughts.

The name that he had written down on the back of the envelope was this: *Gwendolyn Thorpe*.

He turned the light off, rolled over, and was soon asleep, dreaming peaceful and remarkably unmurderous dreams.

Kemble was waiting for him when he arrived in the Dirty Donkey on Sunday night. Peter bought a drink and sat down beside him.

"I'm taking you up on the special offer," he said by way of greeting.

Kemble nodded vigorously. "A very wise decision, if you don't mind me saying so, sir."

Peter Pinter smiled modestly, in the manner of one who read the *Financial Times* and made wise business decisions. "That will be four hundred and fifty pounds, I believe?"

"Did I say four hundred and fifty pounds, sir? Good gracious me, I do apologize. I beg your pardon, I was thinking of our bulk rate. It would be four hundred and seventy-five for two people."

Disappointment mingled with cupidity on Peter's bland and youthful face. That was an extra £25. However, something that Kemble had said caught his attention.

"Bulk rate?"

"Of course, but I doubt that sir would be interested in that."

"No, no, I am. Tell me about it."

"Very well, sir. Bulk rate, four hundred and fifty pounds, would be for a large job. Ten people."

Peter wondered if he had heard correctly. "Ten people? But that's only forty-five pounds each."

"Yes, sir. It's the large order that makes it profitable."

"I see," said Peter, and "Hmm," said Peter, and "Could you be here at the same time tomorrow night?"

"Of course, sir."

Upon arriving home, Peter got out a scrap of paper and a pen. He wrote the numbers one to ten down one side and then filled it in as follows:

1 . . . Archie G.

2 . . . Gwennie.

3 . . .

and so forth.

Having filled in the first two, he sat sucking his pen, hunting for wrongs done to him and people the world would be better off without.

He smoked a cigarette. He strolled around the room.

Aha! There was a physics teacher at a school he had attended who had delighted in making his life a misery. What was the man's name again? And for that matter, was he still alive? Peter wasn't sure, but he wrote *The Physics Teacher, Abbot Street Secondary School* next to the number three. The next came more easily—his department head had refused to raise his salary a couple of months back; that the raise had eventually come was immaterial. *Mr. Hunterson* was number four.

When he was five, a boy named Simon Ellis had poured paint on his head while another boy name James somebody-or-other had held him down and a girl named Sharon Harsharpe had laughed. They were numbers five through seven, respectively.

Who else?

There was the man on television with the annoying snicker who read the news. He went on the list. And what about the woman in the flat next door with the little yappy dog that shat in the hall? He put her and the dog down on nine. Ten was the hardest. He scratched his head and went into the kitchen for a cup of coffee, then dashed back and wrote *My Great-Uncle Mervyn* down in the tenth place. The old man was rumored to be quite affluent, and there was a possibility (albeit rather slim) that he could leave Peter some money.

With the satisfaction of an evening's work well done, he went off to bed.

Monday at Clamages was routine; Peter was a senior sales assistant in the books department, a job that actually entailed very little. He clutched his list tightly in his hand, deep in his pocket, rejoicing in the feeling of power that it gave him. He spent a most enjoyable lunch hour in the canteen with young Gwendolyn (who did not know that he had seen her and Archie enter the stockroom together) and even smiled at the smooth young man from the accounting department when he passed him in the corridor.

He proudly displayed his list to Kemble that evening. The little salesman's face fell.

"I'm afraid this isn't ten people, Mr. Pinter," he explained. "You've counted the woman in the next-door flat *and* her dog as one person. That brings it to eleven, which would be an extra"—his pocket calculator was rapidly deployed— "an extra seventy pounds. How about if we forget the dog?"

Peter shook his head. "The dog's as bad as the woman. Or worse."

"Then I'm afraid we have a slight problem. Unless . . . "

"What?"

"Unless you'd like to take advantage of our wholesale rate. But of course sir wouldn't be . . . "

There are words that do things to people; words that make people's faces flush with joy, excitement, or passion. *Environmental* can be one; *occult* is another. *Wholesale* was Peter's. He leaned back in his chair. "Tell me about it," he said with the practiced assurance of an experienced shopper.

"Well, sir," said Kemble, allowing himself a little chuckle, "we can, uh, *get* them for you wholesale, seventeen pounds fifty each, for every quarry after the first fifty, or a tenner each for every one over two hundred.'

"I suppose you'd go down to a fiver if I wanted a thousand people knocked off?"

"Oh no, sir." Kemble looked shocked. "If you're talking those sorts of figures, we can do them for a quid each."

"One *pound*?"

"That's right, sir. There's not a big profit margin on it, but the high turnover and productivity more than justifies it."

Kemble got up. "Same time tomorrow, sir?"

Peter nodded.

One thousand pounds. One thousand people. Peter Pinter didn't even *know* a thousand people. Even so . . . there were the Houses of Parliament. He didn't like politicians; they squabbled and argued and carried on so.

And for that matter . . .

An idea, shocking in its audacity. Bold. Daring. Still, the idea was there and it wouldn't go away. A distant cousin of his had married the younger brother of an earl or a baron or something . . .

On the way home from work that afternoon, he stopped off at a little shop that he had passed a thousand times without entering. It had a large sign in the window—guaranteeing to trace your lineage for you and even draw up a coat of arms if you happened to have mislaid your own—and an impressive heraldic map.

They were very helpful and phoned him up just after seven to give him their news.

If approximately fourteen million, seventy-two thousand, eight hundred and eleven people died, he, Peter Pinter, would be *King of England.*

He didn't have fourteen million, seventy-two thousand, eight hundred and eleven pounds: but he suspected that when you were talking in those figures, Mr. Kemble would have one of his special discounts.

Mr. Kemble did.

He didn't even raise an eyebrow.

"Actually," he explained, "it works out quite cheaply; you see, we wouldn't have to do them all individually. Small-scale nuclear weapons, some judicious bombing, gassing, plague, dropping radios in swimming pools, and then mopping up the stragglers. Say four thousand pounds."

"Four thou—? That's *incredible*!"

The salesman looked pleased with himself. "Our operatives will be glad of the work, sir." He grinned. "We pride ourselves on servicing our wholesale customers."

The wind blew cold as Peter left the pub, setting the old sign swinging. It didn't look much like a dirty donkey, thought Peter. More like a pale horse.

Peter was drifting off to sleep that night, mentally rehearsing his coronation speech, when a thought drifted into his head and hung around. It would not go away. Could he—could he *possibly* be passing up an even larger saving than he already had? Could he be missing out on a bargain?

Peter climbed out of bed and walked over to the phone. It was almost 3 a.m., but even so . . .

His Yellow Pages lay open where he had left it the previous Saturday, and he dialed the number.

The phone seemed to ring forever. There was a click and a bored voice said, "Burke Hare Ketch. Can I help you?"

"I hope I'm not phoning too late . . . " he began.

"Of course not, sir."

"I was wondering if I could speak to Mr. Kemble."

"'Can you hold? I'll see if he's available."

Peter waited for a couple of minutes, listening to the ghostly crackles and whispers that always echo down empty phone lines.

"Are you there, caller?"

"Yes, I'm here."

"Putting you through." There was a buzz, then "Kemble speaking."

"Ah, Mr. Kemble. Hello. Sorry if I got you out of bed or anything. This is, um, Peter Pinter."

"Yes, Mr. Pinter?"

"Well, I'm sorry it's so late, only I was wondering . . . How much would it cost to kill everybody? Everybody in the world?"

"Everybody? All the people?"

"Yes. How much? I mean, for an order like that, you'd have to have some kind of a big discount. How much would it be? For everyone?"

"Nothing at all, Mr. Pinter."

"You mean you wouldn't do it?"

"I mean we'd do it for nothing, Mr. Pinter. "We only have to be asked, you see. We always have to be asked."

Peter was puzzled. "But—when would you start?"

"Start? Right away. Now. We've been ready for a long time. But we had to be asked, Mr. Pinter. Good night. It *has* been a *pleasure* doing business with you."

The line went dead.

Peter felt strange. Everything seemed very distant. He wanted to sit down. What on earth had the man meant? "We always have to be asked." It was definitely strange. Nobody does anything for nothing in this world; he had a good mind to phone Kemble back and call the whole thing off. Perhaps he had overreacted, perhaps there was a perfectly innocent reason why Archie and Gwendolyn had entered the stockroom together. He would talk to her, that's what he'd do. He'd talk to Gwennie first thing tomorrow morning . . .

That was when the noises started.

Odd cries from across the street. A catfight? Foxes probably. He hoped someone would throw a shoe at them. Then, from the corridor outside his flat, he heard a muffled clumping, as if someone were dragging something very heavy along the floor. It stopped. Someone knocked on his door, twice, very softly.

Outside his window the cries were getting louder. Peter sat in his chair, knowing that somehow, somewhere, he had missed something. Something important. The knocking redoubled. He was thankful that he always locked and chained his door at night.

*They'd been ready for a long time, but they had to be asked . . .*

When the thing came through the door, Peter started screaming, but he really didn't scream for very long.

# FIRST DATE

## JEFF STRAND

"WHAT DO YOU do for a living?" June asked.

Cliff frowned. "I thought I already told you." He glanced around at the other diners in the fancy Italian restaurant to make sure nobody was paying attention to them. "I'm a serial killer."

"Well, that's not really a *job*. It's a hobby, right?"

"No, it's not a hobby! It's the most meaningful thing in my life!"

June nodded. She was thirty-two, according to her profile on the dating site, with long blonde hair, blue eyes, and perfect teeth. Cliff's victims were in their early twenties and brunettes, which he assumed was why June felt safe going out with him. "I didn't mean 'hobby' in a disparaging way. But you can't make a full-time living from being a serial killer, can you?"

"Why not?"

"How do you monetize that?"

"I take their purses when I'm done."

"Then you're a robber, not a serial killer. If you're stealing from them as a trophy, that's one thing, but taking cash from your victims to pay the bills is something a mugger does."

"You're saying I should just leave the money behind?" Cliff asked. "How would that make any sense? Who would do that?"

"A killer who was trying to send the message that it's about the killing, not the income."

"I'm not trying to send a message. It's an outlet for the darkness inside of me. I don't care what anybody thinks."

"That's fair," said June. "In fact, I admire that. You're not trying to play by anybody's rules but your own. If you can make a full-time living stealing purses from your victims, good for you."

Cliff hesitated. "Thank you."

"Why'd you pause?"

"I didn't."

"You totally paused before thanking me."

"So?"

"You're not making a full-time living by stealing their purses, are you?"

"Well, no," Cliff admitted. "Women don't carry much cash with them these days, and using their credit cards would leave a trail. ATM machines have cameras, and I wouldn't want one to snap a picture of me if I entered the wrong PIN number."

"You know—"

"Yes, I know! The 'M' in ATM stands for 'machine' and the 'N' in PIN stands for 'number.' Excuse me for being redundant. Are you always this pedantic?"

"Pretty much," said June. "Most guys find it endearing. You don't?"

"It makes me want to expand my victim pool."

"Rude."

"I was just kidding."

"Uh-huh. We've been here five minutes and you're saying that you literally want to murder me. That's not how you get to second base."

"I was kidding!" Cliff insisted. "If you go out on a date with a serial killer, there's going to be some dark humor. When I take the first bite of my chicken Alfredo I'll probably say something like, 'Mmmm, tastes like human flesh!' even though I'm not a cannibal and have no intention of becoming one."

"Do you say funny quips after you kill somebody?"

"No."

"Never?"

"Nope."

"No puns?" June asked.

"That's only in the movies. In real life, serial killers don't say clever one-liners to their victims. In the moment you're too focused on the task at hand to think of anything witty."

"Makes sense. So when you're lying in bed, replaying it afterward, do you ever think of something you *wish* you'd said? Like when you've had an argument, and you realize the perfect thing you should have said, a real zinger that would've destroyed your opponent, but only after the argument has been over for hours?"

Cliff shook his head. "It wouldn't matter. The person who would've heard me be witty is dead."

"Well, yeah, that's true," said June. "Still, there's something to be said for giving them a little chuckle before they die."

"Not my thing."

"Do you kill them fast or slow?"

"I don't know. Medium, I guess."

"What do you mean by medium?"

"If I just pop up and stab a victim to death, it can be over in, like, twenty seconds. Even faster if I slit their throat. I don't do that, but I also don't take them home and chain them up in a basement so I can have my way with them for the next forty-eight to seventy-two hours. I inject them, drag their unconscious body to my car, drive them to my lair, wake them up, and then torture them to death, but I don't drag it out very long. Fifteen minutes at the most."

"Did you say lair?" June asked.

"Yeah."

June giggled.

"What?" Cliff demanded.

"That just sounds cheesy. Lair. *My lair.* Like you're a comic book villain."

"What should I call it?"

"I don't know. What kind of place is it?"

"A cabin."

"Then call it your cabin. Lair sounds goofy. I would never let a guy put his hand under my bra if he referred to his cabin as his lair."

"Maybe I don't want to put my hand under your bra," said Cliff.

"Your loss."

Cliff picked up his knife. "Maybe instead of putting my hand under there, I'd . . . " He put the knife down. "No, I'd never do that. That's too depraved."

"That was a butter knife."

"I know."

"Were you going to cut off my tit with a butter knife?"

"No! One, I was just using it as a prop. I'd use a normal knife if I was actually going to do it. Two, I wouldn't do it right here in a crowded restaurant. That's how guys like me end up in prison. Three, before I even described what I was going to do, I said that I wouldn't really do it. I'm not the kind of serial killer who would cut off your . . . cleavage."

"My cleavage?"

"You know what I meant."

"How do you cut off a woman's cleavage?" June asked.

"You know perfectly well what I meant!"

"Are you uncomfortable saying the word tit?"

"I choose not to be crude."

"Can you say boob?"

"Yes, I can say it."

"Can you say breast?"

"Of course I can say it," said Cliff. "Anybody can say that. It's not dirty."

"Then say one of them."

"It's not appropriate dinner conversation."

"Say tit, boob, or breast."

Cliff shook his head. "I'm not going to be bullied."

"Okay, I get it," said June. "You kill because you have weird sexual repression issues."

"I do not!"

"Are you a virgin?"

"I don't see where that's any of your business."

"My guess is that you can't get hard because of some seriously messed-up issues in your upbringing, so you use your knife as a surrogate penis. It's literally the only way you can penetrate a woman."

"My God, you really have no boundaries," said Cliff. "We haven't even got our breadsticks yet."

"The breadsticks will be harder than your dick."

Cliff pushed his chair back. "I think we're done."

"No, no, no, I'm sorry," said June. "You're right—I have no boundaries. I shouldn't be talking about your sexual dysfunction. It was tactless. Don't go. I won't make you say tit."

"You've been antagonistic this whole time."

"I know, I know. I'm not a good person. I'll do better. Let's just enjoy our dinner, okay?"

"Okay." Cliff slid his chair back in place. He sighed. "I work at an ice cream shop. That's how I pay the bills. I scoop ice cream for a living."

"There's no shame in that. It's honest work."

"It really is. And it builds muscles. Nobody ever thinks of it as grueling work, but sometimes the ice cream is *really* frozen in those tubs and it takes a lot of effort to scoop it out. You can make it easier by keeping the scoop in hot water, but still, it's a workout."

"And I bet having to deal with customers all day makes you hate humanity, which makes it easier to murder people later," said June.

"No. I don't mind the customers."

"Never thought about scooping out one of their eyeballs and putting it on top of a sundae like a cherry?"

"Nah. I'm not really into the visuals."

"Why don't you get an ice cream truck? You could play creepy music and drive slowly around suburban neighborhoods seeking your next victim."

"I don't kill little kids," said Cliff.

"Well, you said earlier you wanted to expand your victim pool."

"No, I said that you being pedantic made me want to expand my victim pool. And I was kidding. I would never harm a child."

"What if the child was all like, 'You killed my mother!' and had a gun pointed at you, but their hand was trembling while they worked up the courage to pull the trigger, and you knew that if you acted quickly you could stab them to death before they shot you?"

"I wouldn't have to stab them to death. I'd jab the knife in their arm and make them drop the gun."

"Then you're stuck with a kid who knows you killed their mommy."

"We'd work it out."

"How? Threats? Negotiation? Gaslighting?"

"I don't know," said Cliff. "It's a completely ridiculous hypothetical situation. I'd never be so sloppy that a kid could track me down to seek vengeance. But to answer your question, I'd use threats. I'd tell the kid that I was the boogeyman and that I'd climb out from under their bed and eat their face if they ever told anybody what I'd done."

"Damn. Harsh."

"Better than killing them."

"Yeah, you're right. What's taking our breadsticks so long?"

"They're freshly made. You can't rush quality."

"Well, I'm starving. So how many women have you killed?"

Cliff hesitated. "A lot."

"You paused again."

"No, I didn't."

"You totally did."

"I know if I paused or not. I'm the one who would have done it. I know the timing of my own words. Maybe the number is so large that I was trying to count them up in my mind before I answered."

"You can't insist that you didn't pause and then immediately explain why you might have paused."

"You're getting antagonistic again."

"Does it turn you on?"

"No."

"How many victims?" June asked. "Look me in the eye when you answer. And don't do that unconscious thing where you put your hand over your mouth—it's a dead giveaway that somebody is lying. I know all the signs. My dad was a cop."

"My dad was a plumber. I don't know shit about plumbing."

"How many?"

"That's a third-date conversation."

"How many?"

"How many guys have you slept with?"

"Eleven."

"Oh." Cliff looked down at the table. "Is that a lot?"

"I don't know. Is it?"

"I don't know, either. If they were evenly spaced out it's not that many, I guess."

"You're sweating," said June.

"No, I'm not."

"You are. Your face is bright red and you're sweating. Is the sex talk making you nervous?"

"No."

"You blurted out the question without thinking and now you deeply regret it, don't you?"

"No."

"Say tit."

"Why are you so mean?"

"I'm not mean. You tried to deflect my question and it backfired. But it's good for us to talk about fornication—it's healthy to get out of your comfort zone. Have you ever touched a vagina?"

The server brought a bowl of breadsticks to their table. Cliff and June thanked her and took one each.

"Two," said Cliff.

"You've touched two vaginas?"

"I've killed two women."

"That's it?"

"How many have *you* killed?"

"None, but I didn't represent myself as a serial killer. You don't get to call yourself a serial killer if you've only claimed two victims. That's ridiculous. You're just somebody who killed two women."

"How many does it take to become a serial killer?"

"I don't know. Let me Google it." June took out her cell phone and tapped away at the screen. "Three."

"Really?"

"Yes. And they have to be three separate incidents with a cooling down period between them, or else you're technically a spree killer. And if you kill three people at once, it's just mass murder."

"Are you sure? I thought all you needed was to kill more than one person, on purpose."

"That's not what the internet says."

"Oh."

"I can't believe you told me you were a serial killer when you'd only killed two women. That's way worse than using an outdated profile picture."

"My picture's not outdated," said Cliff. "It's from earlier this year."

"Then you had some serious filter action going there. I'm not saying you're ugly at all—I'd totally have let you put your hand under my bra if you'd played your cards right—but you don't look like your picture."

"Neither do you."

June stared at him for a moment. "That was a low blow."

"How was it a low blow? You just got finished saying that I didn't look like my picture, and I said the exact same thing back to you!"

"It's different. I'm sensitive about my looks and you're clearly not sensitive about your own."

"You're a fucking weirdo," said Cliff. "I may have tortured and killed two women, but there is something seriously wrong with you. So how do *you* make a living? We never talked about that."

"Apologize for hurting my feelings first."

"Fine. I'm sorry I said that you didn't look like your profile picture immediately after you said that I don't look like mine."

"I don't accept your apology."

Cliff took a bite of his breadstick. "You know, you're acting like it's not much of an accomplishment to murder two women, but let me remind you that they were both young, attractive brunettes. I couldn't just randomly kill a couple of ladies. I have a *type*. These were women with jobs and families and stuff. They were missed. If I hadn't been careful, we'd be having this date through Plexiglass."

"No, we wouldn't," said June. "I don't date inmates."

"Oh, yes, your standards are soooooo very high when you're out there banging eleven guys in a row!"

"It was eleven guys over fourteen years, and you're sweating again. It's running down your forehead and dripping off the tip of your nose."

"I'm a sweaty person, okay? Some of us have more pores than others."

"You believe that sex is dirty and wicked, don't you?"

"No," said Cliff. "Sex is perfectly fine, if you're into that sort of thing."

"What were you hoping to get out of this date?"

"Nothing."

"Were you planning to kill me afterward?"

"Ha. You wish. You're a blonde and you're too old."

"Then what were you looking for?"

Cliff said nothing. He picked up his napkin and wiped the perspiration off his face.

"Tell me," June said.

"I wanted a friend, okay? Somebody who wouldn't judge me for my atrocities. When you found out that I was a serial killer and still wanted to have dinner with me, I thought you might be the one, but you're just so *unpleasant*. Yes, I think all women are disease-ridden whores and my stomach churns and I break into a cold sweat when the subject of their erogenous zones comes up, but I thought I could get past that to spend time with somebody who liked me the way I am."

June smiled. "That's sweet."

"Do you really think so?"

"Yes."

"It's not pathetic?"

June's smile froze. "It's sweet, okay? Maybe quit interrogating me about it."

"Do you think we could start over?"

"We could, yeah, but I'll be honest—I'll behave the exact same way. You've got innocent blood on your hands, but I'm basically a psychopath. If we started over, I'd still harass you about killing being a hobby and your erectile dysfunction and the fact that you lied about being a serial killer. Then you'd wail about just wanting a friend who understands you and I'd feel a little guilty about laughing in your face but I'd do it anyway."

"I see."

"Look, the honest truth is that somebody who would date a serial killer isn't going to be the highest quality person. I kind of thought that would be obvious and that you would have already managed your expectations, but apparently not. I'm happy to finish this meal with you, but it's going to be more of the same."

"What if I threatened to stab you in the face if you didn't behave?" Cliff asked.

"You won't. You said you have a type."

"That doesn't mean I won't succumb to rage."

"If I feel threatened, I'll mention my boobs and you'll drop into the fetal position."

"Okay, look, as sad as it is to say this out loud, you're the best I'm going to get. Can you at least swear to me that you're not playing the long game?"

"What do you mean?" June asked.

"I mean befriending me just so that I'll kill an enemy of yours who happens to be a twenty-something brunette."

"No, Cliff, I'd never use you like that. I have my limits."

"So is this how our relationship is going to work? You'll keep being shitty to me, but at least I won't have to pretend to be something I'm not?"

"Technically, you were pretending to be a serial killer, which you're not, and you were pretending to not be an ice cream scooper."

"I hate you," said Cliff.

"That's understandable. I don't show it, but I'm filled with self-loathing. I'm also a cutter. That's why you won't see my tits even if they didn't scare you."

"I'm not going to take you along for one of my hunts."

"I'd never ask you to."

"I mean it. You're not my partner. Killing is my special time and nobody is invited but me and my victim."

"I'm cool with that."

"And I didn't want to say it before, but I keep their heads as trophies. I don't do anything to preserve them. I just let them rot in my apartment. They talk to me. They scream."

"That actually makes me feel better. That's something a serial killer would do. You've only killed two women, but you'll get the third soon. I have faith in you."

"Thanks."

"I think we can make this work," said June. "It'll be dysfunctional as hell, yet in a way that's part of the fun, right? I know our meals haven't even arrived yet, but would you like to go on a second date with me?"

"I'd be honored to," said Cliff.

"Perfect. I think this is the start of a great friendship. The serial killer and the necrophile."

"Wait, what . . . ?"

# DOORWATCH

## Kealan Patrick Burke

**For breakfast,** Ned had a single egg and a slice of toast. It was not a big meal, but for years now, big meals had caused him great distress. If he wanted to get through the day without pain, breakfast had to be small enough to circumvent the dyspeptic demon policing his innards. While eating, he perused the morning newspaper, clucking his tongue at the escalating accounts of global and societal decay, and scanning the obituaries to see who he'd outlived. Here was poor Mrs. Jones from around the corner, claimed by ovarian cancer. There was Bob Miller, the mayor of nearby Easterbrook, felled by a heart attack while overseeing the construction of a new wing of the local library. At seventy-six, Ned supposed it wouldn't be long before his own name appeared in one of those little boxes, but the thought was too morbid to linger. Besides, he had work to do. With a small sigh of resignation, he put on his jacket, and headed out into the backyard to start his day.

There was a chill, but not enough to make him regret not wearing his duffel coat. The nylon jacket would do well enough should it decide to rain, a development the dirty sky seemed to be considering.

His yard was not large, the right size for a man who'd never had children or a dog, and for the most part, it looked the same as all the other yards attached to all the other houses on Beech Avenue, where he'd lived since marrying Gretchen in the fall of 1982. The world had changed a lot since then, mostly for the worse, in Ned Barrow's opinion, the *very* worst change being the appearance of his beloved wife's name in those obituaries four years ago when, with no warning at all, she went to sleep next to him and didn't wake up. The other change was the appearance of the door at the end of his yard where once there had only been a low hedge separating his lot from the alley that ran between his house and the Radcliffes'. Whereas Gretchen had been there and then wasn't, the door hadn't been there and then was, and neither development had pleased him, though he could have lived easier with the latter than the former.

The door was tall and heavy and paneled and painted jet black. It stood without a wall to hold it up and was not visible from the alley. Not because anything was in the way. It just wasn't there when you looked at it from that angle. Nor could it be seen from the sides. It existed only when you sat before it, and that's why the red chair was there. It was a simple wooden chair, much like the one he had at the kitchen table, only his was white (or used to be). Painted on the seat was a six-fingered white hand. Each finger was of equal length, and there was an open black eye in the middle of the palm.

Shuddering off the infiltration of the chill, Ned took a seat, crossed his legs, and watched the door, same as he had every day since the door first appeared. This was his job. Nobody had instructed him to do it. Nobody had ever said a word. If the neighbors on both sides of his house noticed the door, they had never let on. Perhaps only *he* saw it. Perhaps he'd gone mad. He didn't know, but it hardly made much difference, because Ned knew he must watch the door to make sure nothing came out. This information hadn't been passed down to him from some spectral higher power. He'd received no instructions or correspondence at all. He'd simply emerged from his home one fine autumn morning, saw the door and the chair, and immediately knew what had to be done, so he did it. It had come as an automatic impulse, like putting your hands out to break your fall.

That was two years ago, and since then he'd never doubted the importance of this task because he knew if he didn't do it, something might sneak through that door and do something terrible. To whom, he didn't know, but that was unimportant too. Only the job mattered, not the whos and whys of it all.

One day a police officer poked his head over the hedge, three feet from the door he clearly couldn't see. He looked concerned.

"Hello, sir," he said.

"Hello," Ned replied.

"Everything all right?"

"I think so. Just watching the door."

The policeman squinted at the back door to Ned's house, some twenty feet behind where he sat.

"Not that one," Ned said.

"Which one then?"

Ned nodded at the air in front of his face. "This one here."

Irritation scrunched the policeman's face. "Are you trying to be funny?"

"No. You asked me what I was doing, and I told you."

"There's no door there."

"Yes there is, but you can only see it from here."

"Have you been drinking today, sir?"

"Haven't touched it in twenty-six years."

"Medication?"

"Antacids for my stomach. Cream for foot fungus."

"But you're out here looking at an invisible door."

"No, sir. I can see it plain as day."

"So if I come around there where you are, you're telling me I'll see it too?"

"I think so, yes."

With a shake of his head and a slight grin, the policeman sidled through the gap in the hedge and must have sensed the door even though he couldn't yet see it, because he moved around it.

"Well?" Ned asked.

The policeman stood next to him, turned toward the door, and went rigid. His breath escaped him in a low hiss, and then he nodded. "You must watch it, make sure nothing gets out."

"Yes, I know."

"It would be terrible if it opened. You must make sure it doesn't open. It makes my mouth hurt. My fillings are singing. You will stay here, won't you?" There was terror in his voice. "You must make sure nothing comes out." A moment before, he'd assumed the old man a loon. Now, he acted as if he'd been aware and lived in terror of the door his whole life. "I can't bear to look at it," he said, and then was gone, back out into the alley, his face white as a sheet.

The old man went back to watching the door.

It wasn't always an easy job. The door required vigilance and that often came at the cost of his personal comfort. It was impossible to watch it all the time, of course. He had to blink, sometimes to sneeze, but he knew, the same way he knew all the other things about the door that he'd never been told, that such perfectly human moments were allowed. At least, by whatever forces had assigned him the doorwatch. Humans, on the other hand, were not always so forgiving.

One Saturday afternoon, he found himself needing to go to the bathroom. Usually, it was enough to go once in the morning, again at noon, and then once or twice more after sundown, but he was getting older and his bladder was tired. Nearby was the empty 7-Up bottle he'd drained since coming out here at 8 a.m.—he found it most effective in calming his sour guts—and that seemed like a fine solution, so he unzipped himself, aimed his hose into the bottle, and relieved himself. A moment later, he heard a gasp and looked up to see Mavis Harkin from four doors down gawking in horror at him over the hedge.

"You dirty, filthy old man!" she screamed, and hurried away. Twenty minutes later, the cops were at his door, and because he could not abandon his post, they were forced to come around to the hedge and interrogate him, which irritated them greatly. Again, they maneuvered around the door without seeing it.

"Mavis is a busybody," he told them. "She'd die if she didn't have gossip to keep her heart thumping."

"She says you exposed yourself to her."

"Nonsense. I needed to go to the bathroom."

"And why didn't you?"

"I can't get up from here until the sun goes down," he explained. "I don't know how I know, but those are the hours. One minute earlier and something might slip through."

Unimpressed, they tried to haul him in for indecent exposure, but as soon as their hands found him, their radios squawked. Through them, Ned recognized the voice of the policeman he'd spoken to weeks before: "Leave him alone. That man must not be removed from his post. There will be hell to pay if he is interfered with in any way."

Confused, the police officers turned to leave, and that's when they saw the door for themselves.

"Jesus," said one, shrinking away from it. "Where did that come from?"

"I don't know, but I'm not waiting around to see what's on the other side of it," said the other, and they made themselves scarce.

Ned made sure to be more discreet with his use of plastic bottle toilets from that day forth.

For six years Mr. Barrow watched the door. He'd become something of a local celebrity, though in a town like Morrow, celebrity status was earned simply by doing anything out of the ordinary, like mowing the lawn after dark. The police had long since stopped paying him visits, and Mrs. Harkin never again passed by the hedge. Pastor Markham did come to visit one sunny Sunday afternoon, perhaps concerned that his one-time parishioner had found a better sermonizer. Ned assured him he had not.

"Thankfully, you don't always need to come to God. God can come to you. I wonder if you might pray with me?" Markham asked, his kind eyes like watery jewels in the sallow mask of his sickly face. Everyone was getting old and sick, it seemed. Ned would have liked to blame the door, but the only enemy here was time. No amount of watching could keep *that* from sneaking in. Thus, although he thought prayer a waste of time, he agreed to the pastor's request. Enthused, Markham knelt in the grass before him and proceeded to quote scripture. Ned's faith had died with the death of his wife, the appearance of the door, and the conviction that whatever waited on the other side of it was as far removed from God as it was possible to get. He watched only for the devils now with no illusions that there was a celestial force to thwart them should they deign to breach the divide.

When the sermon was over and Markham saw the door, he stared inscrutably at it for almost an hour, muttering desperate prayers under his breath. Eventually he turned to look at Ned, and there was a great sadness on his face. "God's not in there at all," he wept. "Only shadows. What if they wake up? What if they creep through? You must not lower your guard, Ned. Promise me you won't. What will they do to us if you do?"

The old man had long considered this. He was meant only to watch the door. He had no idea what he was supposed to do if it opened. He hoped it never did. And if he died, he supposed someone else would be recruited to act as sentry, in his yard or their own. But if, *if* he should still be here when the door opened, was he meant to rush it and slam it shut, put his weight against it until the clamoring died down? He didn't think so, and could only trust that when the time came, he would know what to do, just like he'd known to watch the door in the first place without anyone giving the command.

He grew older and he grew sicker. A doctor summoned by one of his neighbors found him slack in his chair one winter morning. Wrapped in a heavy blanket, he appeared dead, his eyes at half-mast (but fixed as always on the door), his skin like old wax. He was pneumonic, but refused to be taken to the hospital, though he wondered what would happen if he were removed from his post. Would he awaken in his hospital bed to see the door standing there at the foot of it? The doctor fought him until he noticed the door. Then, like an emotionless automaton, he administered aspirin and anti-inflammatory drugs, armed Mr. Barrow with liquids, which he laid at the foot of the chair, and commanded one of the neighbors to help him hook up a heater via an extension cable threaded through the kitchen window. It was enough to keep him warm, but the recovery took much longer than it might have if he'd allowed himself to be admitted.

"You must stay with us," the doctor intoned. "You must, do you hear me?"

Ned, feverish but forever committed, could only nod.

Some men came around one day. Men he didn't recognize. They told him they were scientists or philosophers or professors or investigators. He was hard of hearing now and most of what they said was nonsense. Besides, it didn't matter who or what they were as long as they had not come to interfere with him. They theorized to themselves for three days about the genesis of the mysterious door. Mr. Barrow did not mind them being there, but he also didn't pay much attention to their ramblings. Occasionally he caught snatches of their pedantic waffling, divined mentions of electromagnetic voids and black holes and interdimensional fractures, but it meant little to him.

"I recall the Abigail Lane case," one of them said, "the house where people would disappear if they went upstairs, but not everyone, and not every time. A most curious case indeed. Selective subtraction. It presupposes an element of sentience, of awareness, of *purpose*. When I think of the disappeared, it is not with sadness, but envy. I, and I'm sure the rest of you will agree, want to know what they *saw* on the other side. I suppose it's much the same as wanting to see the face of God, assuming he is anything other than our own creation." Hums of agreement and then someone mentioned The Bermuda Triangle and the discussion became heated.

Ned watched the impassive black surface of door.

They poked and they prodded with their tools and their instruments, grumbling when the door wouldn't show up on film or video, complaining when it wouldn't yield like some suburban sword in the stone when they tried to open it.

The sun went down while they spoke. With great difficulty, for his joints were so badly atrophied from so much time spent in the red chair, it was almost impossible to walk unassisted, he rose and went inside, leaving the heater behind to warm the men while they spoke, which they did, until the sun came up again.

Soon, they would be gone.

He began to fear his death, only because he did not know what was to happen in his absence. The confidence that there were measures in place to compensate for his removal had started to erode. Moreover, he thought he might *miss* the door. Watching it had given him a sense of purpose in the vacuum of his wife's passing. It had subsumed his grief, replacing it with an obsession that was simple on the surface and unfathomable underneath. It had become a symbol of the unknown, a talisman of the mysteries of life and death and beyond, and of stalwart obstinance, for while he and the world around him faded and grew old and weary, the door had stayed the same, stolid, and unyielding.

Other times it occurred to him that maybe he had wasted his life. What if, after all the fear and dedication and wondering, it was nothing more than a simple door? What if the only unknowable void that had appeared was the one inside himself, a void it was now much too late to fill? What if it was *nothing at all*?

At around noon on July 8th, with the sun beating mercilessly down upon him, the air shimmering in the heat, and the houses deathly quiet around him as his neighbors sought solace in the shade, Ned Barrow fell asleep. It was not for long, perhaps twenty seconds, long enough for his head to nod once, twice, then again as the safety net tried to drag him back to wakefulness and then he jolted awake, startled that he had fallen asleep at all. He was eighty years old now though and had long ago earned the right, even if the gods of some unknown universe didn't agree, to sleep whenever he damn well liked.

Disgruntled, he squirmed in his seat, wincing at the protest of every joint and muscle and bone, and resettled himself. Parched and sunburnt, he reached down for one of the three plastic bottles of water in the grass beside the chair, and glanced toward the door.

It was ajar. Just a touch.

Eyes widening in horror, Barrow scaled a mountain of paralysis until he was standing unsteadily upright, arthritic agony bedamned.

He hadn't heard the doorknob turn. Hadn't heard the click of the latch releasing. No springs, no hinges, no creaks or groans. Nothing. And yet there it was, barely open but open enough to hammer an ache into his heart and panic into his chest.

"No," he whispered. "No, I was here." But even as he thought it, he knew simply being there had never been enough. He was supposed to *watch*.

Perhaps there was still time. Perhaps if he moved in a manner that belied his age, he could slam that door shut on whatever nightmare awaited on the other side, ready to heave itself into the world. Perhaps, perhaps. He shuffled, he hobbled, he jogged, and lurched until his right elbow connected with the door. He expected resistance, imagined he felt something push against the other side, but then it shut with a satisfying click, and he almost wept with relief.

It didn't last long.

"What if it's out?" he asked aloud, and looked around in a panic.

The sun still shone, heating the sweat on his brow.

Somewhere a crow cawed.

The crickets still sawed their legs in arhythmic lullaby.

The cicadas trilled in the trees.

Normal. It was just a normal day. Nothing had been given the time to ruin it.

*But then, who opened the door?* he wondered.

As he made his way back to the chair, the sun seemed to wobble. Ned blinked, sure it was his eyes, but then looked down at his shadow and saw there was more than one. There were several of them, in fact, growing from his feet, which was curious because the sun was before him, hovering like a blazing coin above his roof. Each one of those shadows, supposed offshoots of himself, was a more distorted version of the other. Some had claws, others had tentacles, a few had wings, and they were clawing and tearing blackly, soundlessly at each other, at him, but he felt nothing. Nothing but the strength slowly draining from his body as the truth dawned on him.

*It was you, you old fool.* You *opened the door.*

No, he'd never have done that.

He swallowed and felt something like a fist uncoil inside his throat, both inspiring and obstructing his vomit as another something stirred inside his stomach. Quickly, knees protesting the urgency, he turned and hurried back to the door. *I opened the door,* he thought in horror, as unknown things began to wrestle for dominance inside him and something enormous momentarily blocked out the sun, casting the world into darkness brief and cold.

But no, no it was more than that, and when he reached the door with the whispering undulating shadows mounting inside and around him, and threw the black door open, the truth sucked the last of the hope out of him.

On the other side of the door, he saw his yard, beyond it, his quiet empty house.

*I didn't just open it,* he thought.

And the empty red chair.

I walked *through* it.

The door slammed shut in his face, on the real world, leaving him at the mercy of this strange new one, whichever world it was, as the sun flickered and died.

Then there was only the suffocating dark and the sound of gleeful things rushing to bid him welcome.

# PICTURES OF A PRINCESS

## a fable

KRISTOPHER TRIANA

"HONEY, WHY DON'T you go with her?"

Jeff heard his wife's words, but his mind couldn't process them. It was more than the summer heat slowing his reaction to Connie, more than the exhaustion caused by standing in long lines beneath the Santa Cruz sun. Sherri's tiny hand went into his and he gripped it, wondering which of them was more nervous, he or his daughter. He'd gone dry-mouthed just at the sight of the blonde before them. Now that Connie's words were sinking in, the thought of getting closer to Princess Abigail made his stomach shudder as if filled with horseflies.

"Go on," Connie encouraged, holding her phone sideways to take a picture. "Go on, Sherri. Daddy's coming with you."

A shy smile plumped Sherri's cheeks. She wasn't afraid of the blonde in the Princess getup, just bashful when it came to new people. Princess Abigail was Sherri's favorite, whether in storybooks or animated film. Going to The Tulip Tower was half the reason they'd made this trip to Fairytale Land, an amusement park that was part Disney World and part renaissance fair. It was Sherri's sixth birthday and *The New Adventures of Princess Abigail* had recently been turned into a cartoon series. Jeff had watched it many times; sometimes with his daughter, and other times alone at night, after everyone else had gone to bed. But *that* Abigail was just a digitally enhanced drawing. The one who sat upon the golden throne was real flesh and blood.

Sherri pulled him forward, having already started walking toward the princess now that his presence had given her courage. Jeff shuffled in his sandals, holding his breath as they moved past a rainbow of tulips besetting the velveteen row. All the people waiting in line behind them seemed to disappear—the cacophony of excited children, crying babies, and grumbling parents falling mute as Jeff entered a strange state, awake but dreaming.

"She's a princess, Daddy," Sherri explained. "A *real* princess."

It embarrassed Jeff to realize he believed her.

When they reached the throne, the park actress portraying Abigail smiled at Sherri but didn't give Jeff so much as a glance. This disappointed and relieved him at the same time. She was the sort of beautiful that hurts a man to look at, the longing and desire strong enough to feel like a physical blow. That she was dressed in the pretty baby blue princess gown and twinkling tiara only intensified the sensation of loss.

"What's your name, sweetie?" Abigail asked.

Jeff blinked, rocked by his envy of his daughter.

"I'm Sherri," she replied softly, still shy but smiling with what remained of her baby teeth.

"How old are you?"

"I'm six! Today's my birthday." She turned to Jeff. "Right, Daddy?"

When his daughter looked at him, Princess Abigail did too, for the first time. His heart fell into his stomach with a souring splash. The woman's eyes were like topaz, the soft skin of her face as pale as winter flurries. Her smile was warm. If it was forced, the act was convincing.

"That's right," Jeff managed. "Six. Today's her birthday."

He winced internally, feeling like an imbecile for repeating his daughter's words instead of coming up with something more engaging. Abigail turned back to Sherri. He'd blown his chance.

The princess asked his daughter how she was enjoying the park and other rehearsed trivialities, humoring her with the sort of banal questions adults always ask children. Once again, Jeff lost track of what was being said. When Abigail leaned forward, he stared at a curl of golden hair as it fell across her breasts. He tried to imagine the princess pulling down the cups of that dress for him and found it was easy. The breasts would be the type that faced slightly outward, pointing away from her body, smelling of rose peddles and just as soft.

Connie called to him three times before he snapped back to the real world. When he turned back to his wife, she shooed him away with a wide grin, the laugh lines of her face making her look so much older to him than she had just moments ago.

"Get in there," Connie said with a giggle.

He blushed, thinking—ridiculously—that she meant *get inside* Abigail. His wife pointed and he saw Sherri sitting on the princess's lap, all toothy smiles. Princess Abigail was waving him forward for the picture.

"Don't be shy," the princess joked. "I don't bite."

But he liked to imagine she would.

Sherri was still talking about Abigail when they went to dinner, and Jeff was still thinking about her. She'd been so perfect, and exact replica of the illustration of Princess Abigail in *Fables from the World of Nether*, the book he'd had as a child. In the newer books Sherri had, the princess was essentially the same, but the artwork (instead of being hand-drawn and lifelike the way his childhood book had been) was more cartoonish—the head too big, eyes too big, elbows too pointy. His book had made Princess Abigail look real; Sherrie's book made her look like she belonged on a cereal box.

The animated series was the same, the character being ripped out of royalty-free fairytales and capitalized on by a single entertainment conglomerate. Jeff wished he still had his copy of *Fables from the World of Nether*. But even if he were still in possession of it, the illustrations of Abigail would be long gone. When he'd drawn closer to puberty, he'd ripped them out of the book and carried them folded in his pocket so he could look at them any time he desired. One day he'd forgotten to remove them from his jeans before tossing them in the hamper. Mom washed them and in doing so washed away his princess. And he'd never been able to find another copy at libraries, bookstores, or even online. A tale truly as old as time, Princess Abigail's story was available in countless volumes but the artwork that had made him fall in love with her had vanished, taking part of him away with it.

"What a day we've had," Connie beamed. Sherri was on her lap now—*a lesser lap*, Jeff thought. "And to think we get to do it all again tomorrow!"

They'd bought a full weekend pass and were staying at the attached hotel. Now that they'd spent a day in the park, he and Connie agreed three days was overkill. Fairytale Land wasn't as big as Universal or Disneyworld. At least there were some new shows on Saturday. Not that they'd entertain him much.

*Unless she's in them.*

"And what great pictures," Connie said, flipping through her phone. She giggled. "Except for Daddy. I think he was tired here, huh, Sher?"

Sherri giggled too and Connie turned the phone so he could see the photo. He sat on a fake boulder beside Princess Abigail, who held Sherrie in her lap. Though the two of them were beaming at the camera, Jeff's head was turned toward them instead.

Connie showed it to Sherri again. "I guess he just liked seeing *his* little princess with a big princess, huh?"

Jeff waited for a knowing glance from his wife, but it never came. She hadn't known what he'd really been looking at. In her eyes, they were having a jovial family vacation, nothing more. Jeff wasn't preoccupied by carnal thoughts about an amusement park princess half his age. He'd just gotten too much sun and too much greasy carnival food.

But he knew the truth and it was bitter. The way he was feeling now, he'd give up his wife and daughter for one night in the enchanted forest between Abigail's legs. He almost snickered at the thought but drowned it with another gulp of beer. The glass empty, he motioned to the waitress for a third. Now his wife's eyes *did* hold judgment, telling him he'd had enough without having to say it aloud.

"Just one more," he said.

The room had two queen beds. After Sherri fell asleep in hers, Jeff cozied up to Connie, pressing his crotch into her backside as he spooned her. Connie's silky nightgown rode up a little as his erection formed, poking out of the fly in his boxers.

She inched away. "Honey, no."

"She's fast asleep. We'll do it nice and quiet under the blanket."

"No, Jeff. Not now. Not here."

"Then let's go to the bathroom where we can lock the door. We can take a shower together like we used to and—"

"I already took one, Jeff, remember? Besides, I'm tired."

Jeff would have been too, had Princess Abigail not energized him. His mind was racing, loins stirring like a bubbling cauldron. He pressed into his wife's backside again and fantasized of Abigail curling down the bra cups of that blue gown, her breasts coming free and her squeezing them together in her long, white gloves. He envisioned the bottom of the dress curling up, revealing the fluffy petticoat and matching white stockings beneath, the petticoat's ruffles shifting as she closed and opened her legs. *Peek-a-boo.*

Connie turned to face him. Without her makeup she looked wan and waxen. She almost reminded Jeff of his mother-in-law.

"I said *no*, damnit," she whisper-shouted. "Now go to sleep."

She turned over again, away from him, and he scooted all the way to other side of the bed, bitter now, even angry. He punched his pillow for emphasis and heard Connie sigh. Once he was sure she was asleep too, he went to the bathroom and masturbated, his princess taking him in warm and deep, soft gasps of pleasure escaping her, that angel-blonde hair so long it wrapped about his entire body like a rhumba of boa constrictors. When he ejaculated into the sink, his mind suddenly betrayed him and he thought of Connie, lying beneath the bed he and Princess Abigail fucked upon, caught between the mattress and the box spring and crushed to death by every thrust.

Unable to sleep, Jeff went downstairs to the bar. It seemed this was the one part of the whole place that wasn't pretending it was the 16th century. There were some decorations keeping to the theme of the park—shields and swords mounted on walls, plastic ivory clinging to pillars—but Aerosmith was playing on the jukebox, and everyone was dressed in modern clothes, even the staff. Jeff bellied up to the bar and took a stool, running one hand through his hair. Once it had hung nearly to his shoulders. Now it was just beginning to thin. He'd thought of beer on the way down in the elevator, but seeing the glimmering bottles of bourbon behind the bar changed his thirst. The male bartender fetched him a cocktail and Jeff spun sideways on his stool, people watching.

And there she was.

Or at least he thought it was her. The overdone makeup was gone, as was the Fairytale Land gown and tiara. Worst of all, the yellow hair was now a dark russet, like copper stains and old blood. *A wig?* But despite these changes there was no mistaking her face. She still looked like the illustration that was his guide when teenage hormones had confused him. That image had comforted him when he heard his father beating the living shit out of his mother. Jeff would hide in the cabinet beneath the kitchen sink and pet the fine paper, its softness helping him breathe.

This Abigail's pallor had not just been talc or something worn at the park. It was real. As real as the lithe body he could now see more of. The top was low cut, offering a sweet cavern of cleavage, and the jeans were tight as flesh. They stretched against her thighs as she sat at the other end of the bar and when she waved hello to the bartender Jeff saw the tattoos the white gloves had covered up by day. A diamond stud pierced one nostril.

Jeff leaned in and stretched his ears but was unable to hear the conversation she made with the bartender. It was brief, but they clearly knew each other in a chummy way. Jeff wondered if she'd ever sucked his cock. He finished his drink and motioned the son of a bitch over.

"Get me another."

The bartender grinned. Was he being friendly or was he mocking Jeff? When he returned with a refill, Jeff tossed him a buck.

"Who is she?" Jeff asked, the whiskey getting the better of him.

The bartender followed his gaze to Abigail. "Oh, she works here. You probably recognize her from the park."

"Princess . . . " But he couldn't finish. He felt suddenly sophomoric, too vulnerable.

"She plays a lot of characters. Sometimes she's a princess, sometimes a witch or a—"

"A *witch*? I find that hard to believe."

The bartender shrugged. "She pulls it off."

Another patron approached and the bartender quickly pocketed Jeff's tip and walked away, leaving him feeling as if he'd been ripped off somehow. This patron also blocked his view of Abigail, so Jeff took his drink and walked over to the end of the bar where she was sitting. His courage surprised him. He doubted he would be so bold if she were still dressed in her gown and gloves and pett—

He stumbled slightly, more from a dent in the tile than drunkenness. He had a buzz, but it was not paying attention that had tripped him up. His eyes were on the princess. Now hers were on him. For a moment he just stood there, those glimmering blue eyes cutting through him like the medieval daggers on the wall behind her. He placed one elbow on the bar, leaving one empty stool between them.

"Hey there," he said with a smile.

Her return smile was merely polite, the smile of a female employee stuck with a flirtatious male customer. She wasn't on the clock, but still had to act like it. She gave him a quick nod of hello and then took out her phone, tapping on it as a deterrent to further interaction with him. Jeff understood all of this, but still proceeded, unsure what he expected to gain but riding the strange whim anyway.

"Remember me?" he asked.

She gave him a second glance. "Sorry, no. Should I?"

Jeff wondered if she was lying to discourage him or if he was really that forgettable. He could believe both.

"Me and my daughter? Sherri? The one celebrating her birthday?"

She shrugged, elbows on the bar, holding up the phone to stare at. "Sorry, but I talk to lil' girls like that all day long and you'd be surprised how many of 'em are here 'cause it's their birthday."

He noticed a difference in her voice. Her tone was deeper than it had been in the land of Tulip Tower. There her voice had been high and flighty with a slight British accent, properly enunciating each word. Now her words tumbled out like trash from an overturned barrel. Comparatively, she seemed almost ghetto, maybe with a touch of hick.

"I got my picture with you too," he said.

She nodded as if to say *yeah, lots of parents do*. The bartender brought her cocktail and she smiled up at him, saying something soft and low Jeff couldn't make out. She gave the bartender a wink and he touched her arm briefly before heading toward Jeff, causing his stomach to swarm with those horseflies again.

"How you doin', bud?" the bartender asked.

Jeff cleared his throat. "What do you mean?"

"Just asking if you need something."

Jeff wanted to tell him he knew damned well what he needed and so did the princess. But the bartender was younger than Jeff and strong-looking, probably one of those surfers that littered the beaches like hermit crabs.

"I don't think I catch your meaning," Jeff managed.

The bartender pointed at Jeff's glass. Nothing but ice left. This hadn't been a jab after all. He handed the bartender the glass and he scurried away again. When Jeff turned back to Princess Abigail, she wasn't there. Jeff scowled. The bartender had created a diversion. Jeff threw enough money on the bar to cover his tab and walked away before the bartender could turn around. He scanned the bar and spotted Abigail's cute little backside swaying as she walked through the side entrance and out to the poolside tiki bar. Jeff strode in defiance, following her into the night.

Dark faces spoke in the shadows like ghosts, the light of the pool casting everything in an ethereal azure not unlike Abigail's eyes. Small, strung lights guided the way to the bar where she now stood, her back to Jeff. He was only two feet away when she turned around in cloud of cigarette smoke. Her eyes had gone black with night.

"Can I help you with something?" she asked sharply, the customer courtesy gone.

He struggled for words, coming up with only one. "Abigail . . . "

They stared at each other then, the princess looking him up and down. She smirked and shook her head. "Okay. C'mon."

She walked by him, and Jeff followed, a puppy with its master. Leading him to a table furthest from the bar, she sat down and crossed her legs.

"Well?" she said.

He took the other seat. Abigail breathed more smoke and slowly spun her drink, the bronze alcohol catching the light of the pool, making it glitter with murky stars.

"Buy you a drink?" he asked, stupid.

"Not yet."

"What're you having?"

"It's called a zombie."

Jeff nodded. "That for when you're a witch?"

"No. That's for when I'm me."

His frown turned upside-down, just like she sang about on her show.

"I knew it," he said. "The witch thing is just, like, an act."

She didn't reply. Instead, she blew smoke rings and put her feet up on the extra chair. Black boots with tall heels covered her up to the knee.

"I *have* seen you before," she said. "Yeah, sure. Seen you many times. Not just here, but at Disneyland. I was Tinkerbell then. There's a scene in *Peter Pan* where she gets stuck in a keyhole. There's a lift of her skirt and in that moment she's totally helpless." She took a long drag and exhaled. "You like that."

Jeff's eyebrows drew together. "I do?"

"Yeah, you do. Even if you don't know it. Even if you've never been to Disney or even seen *Peter Pan*."

"How do you know what I like?" he instantly regretted saying it. It sounded too standoffish. "I mean . . . what do you mean?"

Abigail flicked her butt away and it plunked into the deep end of the pool. No one seemed to notice.

"How's your wife?" she asked.

Jeff bit his lip and looked away.

"Well then," Abigail said, "how's your daughter? You did say it was a little girl, right? Not a son but a daughter. How's she?"

Jeff turned back to her. "I love my daughter."

"I'm sure."

He couldn't tell if she was being sarcastic. He chose to believe not.

"So," Abigail said, "how's she tonight?"

"Enjoying our vacation. Happy to have met you. Probably dreaming of you right now."

"And not alone in that, huh?"

Jeff surprised himself by saying, "Yeah. Definitely not alone in that."

A waitress broke the sudden silence between them. "Last call."

Abigail ordered two zombies and mercifully the waitress went away. Jeff wondered about the order. Was she encouraging him or just getting two for herself?

"They don't let us take 'em home, you know," she said.

He blinked. "What?"

"Not just the wigs and ball gowns. Even the big bear and rabbit costumes come back soiled when they leave park property. Nobody takes 'em home with them."

"That's too bad."

"Is it?" She took out another cigarette and Jeff marveled at how her tight jeans hadn't crushed the pack.

*More magic*, he thought.

The waitress dropped off the zombies and scurried into the night to end her shift. Jeff hadn't realized it'd gotten so late. Abigail took one glass and sipped, not telling Jeff if he was welcome to the other. When he took it, she said nothing about it.

"That kid in you," she began, "he's not comin' back. You know that, don't you?"

Jeff swallowed hard. "I do."

"Time hurts enough. Every step backward just causes people more pain."

"I know that too."

She paused. "Then you must enjoy pain."

He raised the glass and said, "Guess I do."

She looked out at the night world that had swallowed them. The other tables had emptied, leaving only the patrons sitting at the bar. He was alone with Abigail here in this blue phantasmagoria, as if they hovered within one giant, blue eye—*her* eye. The zombie was sweet—rum, brandy, youth.

Looking at her profile, Jeff had to choke back a sudden gasp, realizing it was the illustration from the back cover of *Fables from the World of Nether*. Her cigarette smoke replicated the fog of that dreamland the artist had created. She was a white swan, a vision of beauty carved in alabaster. *Does alabaster crack easy*? Jeff had almost forgotten about the back cover of the book. Now he remembered the wet, red stain that had ruined it. He'd seen blood splatter from his mother's mouth so many times. He hadn't realized that would be the last.

"A man can do a serious thing," Jeff said, "but it doesn't always pack any real meaning."

"So can a woman."

"But not a princess. She's not like a regular woman. Everything she does has meaning, purpose."

"And why do you suppose that is?"

"Simple." Jeff leaned in. "*Magic*."

The princess stared at him then, the loveliness shining through despite this ugly guise of nose piercings and tattoos and hooker boots. She hadn't turned back into a pumpkin at midnight. This was a test, a sort of glass slipper. She'd been testing him his whole life.

"Magic is how you know so much," Jeff said, "far more than my wife ever could."

"I don't even know your name."

"But I know yours. Known it since I was old enough to read. And even though the paper cutouts are gone . . . I still carry you."

A smile grew wide upon her face and for one sweet moment in time Jeff thought he'd touched her with his confession. But then the laughter came—the horrible, horrible laughter. She laughed so hard she snorted. He felt suddenly so very small, a child looking for a kitchen cabinet to hide in.

"Why're you laughing?" he said. "It's not funny."

Abigail took a deep breath to steady herself, then tossed back what remained of her drink and got out of her chair.

"No," she said, grinning. "It's really not."

She walked away from the table and Jeff realized they were alone in this darkness now, the lights of the tiki bar having gone out, the patrons and hotel staff having vanished.

*More magic*, he thought.

Jeff got to his feet, following her again, following her all these years. Now that he'd finally come here, having indoctrinated his daughter into loving Princess Abigail enough to convince his wife they had to vacation at Fairytale Land, he wasn't about to let his princess disappear again. She knew the truth. She'd seen it from her tower inside the folds of his book, witnessed everything. Abigail understood all the things he'd been incapable of telling Connie because Abigail had been there for it, been there *for him*.

She opened the gate surrounding the pool and walked out to the rear parking lot of the hotel. The lot and alley were deserted. She approached her golden chariot. It had been transformed into a beige Hyundai, all an illusion. Abigail must have heard his footsteps. She looked over her shoulder but pretended she wasn't looking. She picked up her pace. Then suddenly she was running.

"Don't!" Jeff called out to his princess.

Abigail pressed her magic key (made to resemble a car fob) and two golden orbs came alive at the front of the chariot. She was climbing inside when Jeff took her by the wrist and pulled her back. She struggled against him.

"Put it on!" he said. "I know you have it. You say they don't like you to keep the gowns, but I know the one you wore is your own, Abigail."

"Let go!" She kicked his shin but missed the bone. "Let me go!"

"And go off to Netherland? We'll go together. Just put on the gown. Take off that wig and show me your blonde hair." He pulled at her hair and she shrieked. "You don't have to hide from me. I've never hid from you."

Abigail's scream echoed across the empty lot. It'd been a long time since he'd heard a woman scream like that. Mom had screamed the same way when he'd punished her for drowning his princess in the washing machine. Punished her just like Dad always had, Jeff beating her with his fists and not stopping even after she'd fell unconscious. He'd climbed on top of her and kept on swinging, his arms going back and forth, crushing the bones of her face. His fists seemed to disappear in the pulp. When a glob of blood flew from her mouth it splattered across the book on the nearby end table. *Fables from the World of Nether* was soiled, soiled like a princess gown brought home to be fucked in, coming back to Fairytale Land crusted with semen. The blood wouldn't come off, so Dad threw the book in the trash even as Jeff cried and begged him not to.

"We have to get rid of all the evidence," Dad said. "Anything with blood on it has to go! You don't want to go to jail, do you?" Jeff shook his head. "Then forget the damn book of fairy stories, Jeff. Christ, you're seventeen! Time to grow up! Now help me stuff your mother into the mattress so we can haul it to the dump."

Abigail grabbed his wrists as he yanked at her hair with both hands. Her scalp began to separate and blood spilled down her face, making her look all the more like the back cover of his long lost book. But there was no blonde hair hiding beneath.

"More magic," he grumbled.

He clawed at her arm, wanting to tear away the fake tattoos, but his nails only dug up more flesh, flesh as soft as pages torn from an old book. The princess kicked at him again, going for his groin. He knew what she wanted; it was the same thing Connie pushed away earlier that night. Abigail's jeans were tighter than his. He'd have to get them off first. He punched her in the face, sending out one tooth and breaking another in half, and he could see his daughter's half-toothed smile shining back at him, his two princesses converging before he swung again and again, blinding one of Abigail's eyes. *Peek-a-boo*. He tore the ugly nose stud out of her face. Sprawled across the hood of her chariot, arms spread out to fly the way she did when she got her wings at the end of her fable, Abigail's boots and jeans came off with surprising ease now that she was no longer moving.

She was his sleeping beauty.

And he had more than just a kiss to give her.

When he came out of the bathroom after washing his hands, Sherri was sitting up in her bed. She and her mother had been sound asleep when he'd come back to the room, but now his daughter was wide awake, her feet dancing a little beneath the blanket. He looked at her little face half-hidden by shadow. A smile with missing teeth greeted him.

"I can't sleep anymore, Daddy."

He came over and sat on the edge of the bed. "Too excited?"

"Yeah. I wanna go to Tulip Tower again. Can we do that first?"

"Sure, sweetheart."

"We'll see Abigail again?"

He thought of the broken body he'd left stripped and bleeding in the darkened lot. If not for the magic, he would worry. But not a day went by in Fairytale Land where Princess Abigail wouldn't greet her visitors and take pictures and sign autographs. She'd be there bright and early; no bruises or split lips or nostrils ripped in half. No cracked skull or violated private parts. There was always a princess somewhere, someone to be blonde and pale and perfect in a blue gown and sparkly tiara. Princess Abigail would go on no matter what had happened overnight, no matter how dark the woods or how hungry the big, bad wolf.

"Yes, Sherri. We'll see her again." He touched his daughter's shoulder. "Our princesses are always there for us."

# LAWS OF VIRULENCE

JEREMY ROBERT JOHNSON

## INTERNAL MEMO: 08/07/2010

CASE: F-DPD0758 (CDC NORS-Water Report ID VEC147, Received 08/03/2010 via State Report OMB No. 0920-0004, Submitted by: Dr. Lorena Santos of Pacific Grace Clinic)

ETIOLOGY: Unknown (comparative specimen analysis in progress, genus/species/serotype may require new designations)

CONTAMINATION FACTOR: C-N/A, Unknown

SURVIVAL FACTOR: S-N/A, Deaths can be attributed to case though comparable pathogens have displayed symbiotic behavior

DOCUMENT INSERT: Verbatim transcript of post-containment etiology determination interview with Subject 5 (Matthew Hall). Due to active vector status (transmission mode remains classified as Indeterminate/Other/Unknown although enteric Phase 1 possible) subject interviewed in iso via 2-way audio. DPDx program active/engaged. Elimination & Control team at ready.

Recorded at Director's Request/Classified Confidential 1-A. Speaking: DPD Director Cliff Selzer, Matthew Hall

CS: Hello, Mr. Hall.

MH: [No response]

CS: I'm going to be frank with you, Mr. Hall . . . Can I call you Matthew?

MH: You can call me whatever you want.

CS: Very well, Matthew. I need you to understand the situation we're in right now. How important you are. How much you can help us.

MH: I'm not important. I'm the least important person you've ever met. And I don't give a shit about helping you. And if you don't get me something stiffer than this glass of fucking tap water then I'm not saying a word.

CS: Matthew, I'm afraid that water is all we can provide you right now. But if you cooperate there could be adjustments to your Stay Profile.

MH: You get me a bottle of Maker's and a shotgun. You promise that. Then I'll tell you everything.

CS: You know I can't do that.

MH: I don't know what you can or can't do. I don't even know who the hell you are. You strip me naked. You spray me down with some kind of goddamn fire extinguisher and make me sit in the dark in three smaller and smaller rooms. I thought you were cooking me alive in the last one.

CS: Matthew, that was all for standard decontamination protocol. We're trying to protect you and others.

MH: So am I safe now?

CS: "Safe?"

MH: Decontaminated?

CS: [Long pause] We're not sure, Matthew. That's why it's so important you tell us what you know.

MH: [Garbled] fucking shitbirds. Just let me die. Please.

CS: That's very selfish, Matthew. There are millions of people in this country who don't want to die, and you're putting them at risk. If you won't speak with me, will you at least consider filling out the form we've placed in front of you?

MH: [Sound of pen being thrown across room, striking floor. Sound of Subject 5 expectorating on form CS115.]

BREAK IN RECORDING

MH: Now that's more like it, chief. Aaah, that's more like it.

CS: I suggest you slow down, Matthew. We don't know how alcohol will affect the specimen or its interaction with your body.

MH: [Sound of gulping.] Shit on your specimen, chief. [Sound of belch.] Oh, Jesus, that fucking burns.

CS: It's 100 proof, Matthew.

MH: No, not the booze. That stuff is silky. It's the fucking crawler. Sonofabitch never stops working on me. I knew it. Your precious little detox rooms were a waste. [Sound of fabric rubbing on skin.] See, my mouth is already bleeding. Then I'll get the fucking seaweed eyes. Then you guys will wish you already would've given me that shotgun.

CS: "Seaweed eyes?"

MH: Yeah. It's like lace under the eyes, or like . . . like they're bloodshot but the blood is dark green.

CS: And your wife displayed this condition?

MH: Claire had it first, and then . . .

CS: Then your daughter?

MH: [Long pause. Sound of gulping.] Yeah . . . Myra.

CS: We've performed a full sweep of your apartment, Matthew. We're aware of your loss and I promise you we understand how difficult this must be.

MH: Did you burn them?

CS: No. Our procedure dictates a course other than destruction . . .

MH: Quit fucking around and burn them. Please. Give them that. Claire always wanted to be cremated and . . . I was going to do it myself, before you guys booted in my goddamn door . . . please. It's the last good thing I can do for them.

CS: The sooner we know what you know, the sooner we can honor your request.

MH: Promise?

CS: We will do our best to keep funeral processing in motion.

MH: Well, cheers to that. [Sound of gulping.]

CS: So, at what point did you notice the discoloration in your wife's eyes? And were there any notable signs or symptoms prior to that? Vomiting? Fever? Abdominal cramps?

MH: There are probably some symptoms I didn't even notice. To be honest, we weren't talking that much. I mean, this all happened last week, and it happened so fast. But she was always bitching and crunching on Tums and popping Tylenol, so . . . I mean, running a daycare center is hard work. She used to joke that children could only grow by stealing your energy and happiness. But she liked it, she really did. Hell, she was pretty much raising Myra without me.

CS: Our records indicate you lived together.

MH: [Brief laughter.] Depends on how you define living, chief. We split rent on an apartment and had the same last name, you know... Sometimes I'd take Myra to the park. She was too little to go on the swings or anything, but she liked to smell the flowers and watch the other kids play . . . But Claire would have been the second person, after me of course, to tell you that I'm a piece of shit. A real charity case. So the truth is that I didn't notice how wrong things were until they'd gone way past wrong.

CS: What did you observe first?

MH: Well, I woke up after Claire every day, and I'd make the bed to pretend I was useful in some way, and I noticed some little spots of blood on her pillow. Nothing too serious looking. But then she got home that night and had a hefty cough. Plus, her breath had become pretty toxic. She'd block it with her hand, but the smell would float across the whole room. And this smell, chief, it was like a dead hooker's pussy stuffed with old shrimp. But worse. It crawled into your nose like it was living. She started burning *nag champa* incense, so she must have smelled it too.

CS: Is that when she decided to go to the hospital?

MH: No. Claire is . . . Claire was a tough one. I was starting to feel a little sick, too, and Claire figured we had some food poisoning. It was her birthday a few days before, and I'd been out "job hunting" at the Pussycat Palace. You know the place?

CS: I'm aware of it.

MH: So you've seen Cherry Headrush dance before?

CS: No, Matthew. But I'm aware of many venues and chains because of their prominence on our regional disease vector maps.

MH: Oh. Shit. [Sound of gulping.] Well, I'd flipped for this girl, Cherry. And they'd just extended my unemployment for another three months, so I was feeling flush. Spent almost my whole check in one afternoon, hogging up the lap dances. Milking a cheap beer buzz for hours. And then my cell started vibrating and a reminder message pops up: CLAIRE B-DAY DINNER TONIGHT. Only the "tonight" is spelled like 2-N-I-T-E which means Claire programmed this into my phone so I'd remember. [Long pause.]

CS: Please continue. The food poisoning?

MH: So I'm running late, very buzzed and most of my cash is already in the Pussycat's sterilizer. But I have to try and pull myself out of this, so I hit Chinatown and looked for something fancy to cook up. Chan's Market has a beautiful red snapper on discount, so I cop that, pick up some lemon and capers, and get two fancy chocolate cupcakes at Dreampuff's.

SEE SEPARATE DOCUMENT INSERT FOR RELATED DIRECTOR ORDER: DPDx multi-venue deploy/search/surveil. Full containment authorized. Andolini appointed Team Leader.

CS: Sorry about that break, Matthew. You've been very helpful.

MH: Do I have any choice? Really? I appreciate the second bottle, but you might want to give me a bucket if I'm going to keep going. Although I'd have no problem shellacking your little desk here.

CS: Consider us well-advised. Please continue.

MH: Shit, man . . . it seems obvious, doesn't it? I barely had any time to bake the fish before Claire got home with Myra. I brushed up and changed my clothes and put on some Alicia Keys even though I can't stand that shit. Lit a couple of tea lights I found under the sink. But I still fucked it up. I still fucked it up. [Pause] The fish looked good by candlelight. Looked delicious.

CS: You think the red snapper was the original source of the sickness?

MH: Thing is, I was pulling off the sober act, but I had to burp. And that just ruined it. One hundred percent. Like a strip club came out of my mouth. Claire pegged it, and laid into me, even though Myra was sitting in the room in her little bouncy chair and we'd sworn not to fight in front of her. And I mentioned that, and we tried to enjoy the dinner and pretend that everything was okay and nice and we didn't even notice how raw the snapper was until we'd taken out half of the fish.

CS: So Claire was guessing that the raw fish had given each of you food poisoning?

MH: Yeah. She was toughing it out until Myra got sick, too. Because that didn't make any sense. Myra was still breastfeeding, so she never had any of that nasty snapper. But she was coughing and having the blood speckles just the same.

CS: That's when she visited Pacific Grace, toward the beginning of August?

MH: I think so. I was sort of on my own thing while this was happening. Sleeping on the couch at night. Hiding at Pussycat's during the day. I told myself I was in exile, giving Claire some space to forgive me. But I was really just doing the same old shit. Living in a worn-down strip club booth, paying Cherry to hip-hump me. Hoping that Claire and Myra would start feeling better. That maybe Claire would start feeling so good she'd build up the mojo to finally drop me.

CS: When did you find out she wasn't feeling better?

MH: Well, Pussycat's kind of extradited me back to my family. I was already putting off that rotten jellyfish smell and . . . let's just say there aren't enough dollars to make a stripper let you cough blood in her face. I didn't even see it coming. Just sitting there half-chubbed and dead drunk and BOOM! No tickle in the throat. No warning.

CS: Do you happen to know Cherry Headrush's real name?

MH: You're kidding, right? [Sound of bottle opening/sound of gulping.] All I know is that I was home and starting to feel pretty rotten myself, and I can't imagine how Claire was managing to run the daycare like that. All those little people screaming. "I want. I need. Watch me. Love me." Jesus.

CS: This was the Morning Sun Daycare on Stanton?

MH: Yup. So, Claire stumbles into the house and she and Myra are both coughing and they have those triple-dark circles under their eyes, and seeing them like that makes me feel like I managed to sneak into Hell without dying. Just worthless. No, worse than that—fucking evil. [Long pause] Claire said the lady at the hospital gave them both two I.V. bags to rehydrate them, and that they needed to go back tomorrow for more diagnostics. But she thought it might be a parasite, like one of those squiggly little gut worms you get from eating sushi in Ohio.

CS: Did she suggest you go with them?

MH: Of course. And I was thinking it was the right thing to do. I was starting to feel weak in my bones. But the next morning I wake up and they're already gone and there's a text on my phone saying that they're both "feeling much better." Which was weird, because they'd been coughing like crazy all night. Just brutal sounding. Wet. Like I'd guess TB used to sound.

CS: So . . . a productive cough followed by an apparent return to vigor?

MH: Sure, chief. However you want to call it. It spooked me because I was still under the weather. But I pegged that up in my mind as booze-related immune suppression. All those sauced little white blood cells getting bitch-slapped by the bugs in my system.

SEE SEPARATE DOCUMENT INSERT RE: Viability of ethanol [or variant] ingestion as chemical deterrent to life cycle of [un-named parasite/parasitoid CASE: F-DPD0758].

CS: So when did it become evident that Claire and Myra were still . . . unwell?

MH: [Prolonged sound of gulping.] You want to hear the rest, you get me a loaded shotgun. I promise I'll only fire it once.

CS: Not an option, Matthew.

MH: Okay. Fuck it. I better get the truth out before the goddamn crawler starts telling my story. [Pause/sound of shuddering exhalation.] I knew they were still unwell when I found their tongues. Claire's was in the bed, tucked under a pillow. Dried up already, like jerky. And Myra's . . .

CS: Please, Matthew.

MH: Myra's was in her crib, next to her favorite pacifier, the one with the orange dolphin on the back. And I've got to tell you, chief, between my half-sick, half-drunk stupor and lack of sleep, I felt like I was dreaming. So I did what seemed like the right thing. I threw the tongues in the garbage and kept on tidying the apartment. Like I could organize away what I was seeing. Like I could clean up reality.

SEE SEPARATE DOCUMENT INSERT FOR RELATED DIRECTOR ORDER: DPDx forensic detachment to attain SW Sanitation schedule/potential combing of landfill [use of trailing dogs authorized]. Retention of tissue from Subjects 3 and 4 Top Priority, presence/absence of eggs to be communicated ASAP.

MH (continued): So I had the place pretty spruced, and I was waiting for them to come home. Claire wasn't answering her phone. And my nerves were on four alarm blaze, so I had some bourbon close by, just to keep things mellow until I could figure out what was going on. I'd call her phone. Five rings. Voice mail. Nothing. Take a swig. Five rings. Voice mail. Nothing. And they still weren't home by 9:00 p.m.

CS: Records show you called Claire's mother.

MH: Three or four times. But she never picked up. And I thought about calling the cops, but I knew my speech was slurring by that point. What would I tell them? There was no crime, and they'd probably guess it was just another wife bailing with the kid, leaving the stew-bum behind.

CS: But their tongues? That must have . . .

MH: Can't see that impressing the cops either. Just a way to induce them to pack a straight jacket. Besides, if I mentioned finding their tongues . . .

I'd been on a steady drunk trying to bury that detail, hoping I was just losing my shit.

CS: So when did you next see Claire and Myra?

MH: Never again. I think the night they came home from the doctor's was the last time I really saw them.

CS: Matthew, the chronology we've established shows the three of you were in that apartment for almost two days before we . . .

MH: Before you decided to bust into my place and stop me from finishing my work? Listen, chief, this is hard enough to talk about. So let me lay it out for you without all of your interjections and then we can clear up your questions later.

CS: [Long pause.]

MH: That's more like it. So what I'm saying is that I saw Claire and Myra again, but they sure as shit weren't my Claire and Myra. At some point that night I'd finished my bottle and given up on my phone crusade. I remember thinking, "She finally left me." And I remember feeling so relieved. No one would expect anything from me after that, you know? I'd cop some menial job, enough to service a studio apartment and child support. I'd push for a few weekends a month with Myra, just enough to not feel guilty when I show some stripper a picture of my kid. I think I'd been waiting for a long time for a chance to fall apart.

CS: Matthew, I need to know more about your wife and child, and time is a factor. We have a staff psychologist you can speak with later if you need to get more familial issues off your chest.

MH: Courtesy is a short-lived thing around here, huh, chief? All right then, shitbird . . . So I passed out on the couch, if you can believe it. Noble. Noble guy. And when I woke up, they were sitting at the foot of the couch, both of them, very quietly and . . . holy shit . . . and Claire was nursing Myra, and her head was tilted, and she was staring across the room at nothing, like she was back on Paxil, and they both had those goddamn seaweed eyes. And Claire had both of her breasts out and the one that wasn't in Myra's mouth was . . . it was kind of lumpy, like it had been stuffed with tapioca, and the nipple looked raw, just red meat raw, with these blisters around it, some popped, some filled up with the same dark green that was in her eyes, and . . .

CS: Hold on for a moment please, Matthew.

SEE SEPARATE DOCUMENT INSERT RE: Confirmation of multiple gender-specific intra-species transmission methods as seen in CASE: F-DPD0674. Student population under Sector 6 Quarantine should immediately be grouped same sex for confirmation/testing of all fluids for presence of concurrent microparasites.

CS: Okay, we're back, Matthew.

MH: [Garbled/indistinct vulgarity.] My tongue is starting to feel numb. [Sound of coughing/spitting]. Aw, Christ, chief.

CS: I'd suggest drinking some water. We need you to finish your account.

MH: Yeah, well . . . suggest in one hand and spit in the other and see which one fills up first. [Sound of laughter/sound of gulping/sound of empty bottle set down on table.] What you have to understand is that I thought I was dreaming, seeing Claire and Myra like that. Between the guilt and the hooch, that kind of nightmare fits right in. But then Claire put one of her bony bird hands on my ankle and she turned toward me and smiled. And I swear to God, these two wiry antennae uncurled from in between her teeth and started swaying in the air. So of course I lost my shit. I rolled onto my side and chucked out my guts on the shag carpet, and it's just bile and bourbon and I get that post-puke rush where things feel okay for a moment and I'm thinking I'm awake now and then I turn back towards Claire. [Long pause] She's still smiling at me and this voice comes out of her mouth and says, "Empty. Feed." And she's got her other breast cupped and I swear it's dribbling this shit like fucking wheat grass juice. [Pause] And Myra . . . Myra pulls off of the other breast, or at least her lips move away, but there's something else pushing out of her mouth, something with those same feelers wiggling, and it's latched on to Claire, right on her tit, and it's got these two tiny claws pinched on and its body is pulsing and hunching, and these plates on its back are clicking together and I can see through this thing's belly, where the skin is clear and its guts are filling up green. And Myra's eyes look almost black, but I can still tell they're rolling back in her head . . .

CS: Claire could speak?

MH: They both could. But Myra . . . she didn't have any words yet, so she would smile and her lips would pull back, but all that came out . . . Have you ever seen that footage of dolphins being massacred in Japan? And

Claire's voice was different. There was a lisp, like her mouth was too full, and there was a sort of hissing to it, like cricket legs or . . . [Pause] And the smell that came from them filled up the room. It was like being stuck in the dumpster behind a seafood wholesaler on a hundred-degree day. Made me throw up again.

CS: So why didn't you call 911?

MH: Are you listening to me, chief? This strikes you as a rational response fucking situation? I had no bearings. I asked Claire a question, thinking that this time she'd give me a normal answer in her old, sweet voice and I'd be all the way awake, but it came out with no authority and just made me feel smaller and detached and more alone. But I told her I was worried and that I wondered where she was yesterday and she smiled again . . . I'm thinking that's the only way the thing could move around in there . . . and all she says is, "Work. Feeding." And I say, "You were at the daycare?" She nods and says, "Feeding. Growing. Most will be born." Then she looks down at Myra, and her nose curls up like she's disgusted, and she says, "This one is dying. This one is too small." [Long pause/sound of soft crying.]

CS: Matthew, I'm sorry. I'm so sorry. But the more detail . . .

MH: Details, chief? Go fuck yourself. I did what I did. I tried to save them. I tried to fix it. To fix them before anybody would have to know . . . But it was too late. I could barely stand, but Claire was always pretty frail, and this fucking bug thing had wiped her out. So I tried to help her first and it wasn't too difficult to get her hands belted behind her, but that thing . . . that thing had teeth or mandibles or whatever and Claire started to shake and even with all the lamps in the room turned on my head kept making a shadow over her face and Myra was squealing and stomping her heels down where I left her on the carpet and I couldn't tell where the thing in Claire's mouth ended and the rest of her tongue began and when I cut in with the box knife it started bleeding so bad . . . But for just a moment Claire was looking straight at me, and even with the green lace it looked like her old eyes and then she spit right in my face. Right in my face, and she meant it. And her mouth was half-filled, and I noticed the blood from the thing and my wife wouldn't quite mix, so there's your details chief. Then her lips pulled back and the eyes were still Claire's eyes and she said, "You did this to us."

CS: Matthew, she . . .

MH: She was right. She was right. Even after I managed to finish cutting through, and I'd pulled the goddamn thing out of her face and smashed it under my foot . . . You want more details? The shell of the thing started changing colors and it hissed and sprayed a yellow mist out of its mouth after I set it on the floor. What the fuck does that? Even after I got the thing out of Claire, she still had her eyes trained on me, just bullet-eyes, and she couldn't have hated me any more. And I couldn't fix her, because she was already weak and I don't think she could stop from choking on all that blood. But I thought that Myra . . . [Long pause.]

CS: You didn't try to remove the "crawler?"

MH: I didn't want her to bleed like Claire. So I thought if I could just kill the bug that maybe it would just detach and . . . and I was thinking of how they cook lobsters, and I tried to keep the water in a tin can and hold her over it, but the steam was making everything slick and I couldn't get her mouth open at the same time and . . . so I thought that the burns would heal, you know how they say that the inside of your mouth can heal so fast, and then at least she'd live, and I didn't put the sponge in there for more than twenty seconds, but the thing was hissing and it tried to curl in on itself, and Myra started shaking and making fists and then her eyes were open and they were looking right at me, right into me, and . . .

CS: Matthew?

MH: They were right. There's nothing . . . [Sound of empty glass bottle being shattered.]

CS: Matthew, please. There's no need to . . .

MH: I did this. I did this. I . . . [Sound of Subject 5 collapsing on floor. Sound of wet coughs/exhalations. Faint sound of specimen clicking/squealing from interior of Subject 5. Sound of door opening/boots shuffling/Subject 5 moved to stretcher.]

CS: Goddamn it, [REDACTED]. I said plastic bottles only. Triage?

DPDx: Subject 5 at ISS 75. Both major sources of blood flow to brain severed, trachea punctured. He was committed.

CS: The specimen?

DPDx: Significant damage. Suggest immediate retrieval attempt.

CS: Agreed. Prepare for transfer to Surgical Theater 8, movement protocol in place.

DPDx: Confirmed. [Brief pause.] Director?

CS: Yes?

DPDx: If I didn't know better, I'd think this dead fuck was grinning right at me.

CS: Could be a symptom of the parasite attempting to exit the damaged host. Stay far from his mouth until we've assessed specimen mobility. And let's keep it moving. Perhaps Matthew's got a second chance at fatherhood.

DPDx: [Muffled laughter] Yes, sir. Rolling out.

END TRANSCRIPT

# CURSED OBJECTS

MONA KABBANI

THERE'S A PART of Rachel beneath the skin that makes Adena nervous. She can see it sometimes in her eyes, the black fog twisting just under that hazel hue, ready to pop. It's common in people who are driven by mania. Instantaneous bouts of energy where the world is suddenly conquerable. Where anything is possible. Even for two teenage girls in the midst of a self-led rebellion.

It's one of the reasons Adena is so drawn to her.

And it's also the reason she fears her.

So Adena supposes, of all the pastimes the two could engage in on a Friday night, kneeling over a black jar in Rachel's basement is the mildest. But still, something about the look on Rachel's face disturbs her. Because if anything is possible in Rachel's mind, then the possibility of what she's saying being true excites her.

And this is nothing to be excited about.

"What do you mean *disappear*?"

"Disappear, dead, gone from all existence. Semantics. Who cares? It's all the same thing. Just gone."

Adena shakes her head. "But gone where?"

Rachel frowns. "I just said it doesn't matter."

Rachel opens the lid of the jar. At the bottom, there's a layer of wax and a single wick. Rachel reaches for the matches and lights the wick. The scent of burning fills the air.

"Where did you say you got this from?" Adena asks.

"I didn't. I made it."

Adena bites her lip. Why would Rachel want to make something like this? What gave her the idea?

"Okay, so here are the rules. Pick a name and write it down on a piece of paper. Toss it in, close the lid, and if the name burns up, then that person is gone."

"And if it doesn't?"

"Then they got lucky." Rachel laughs and strikes a pose like she's cursing to the heavens. Her pale fingers decorated with black marker look like art pieces offered up to a god. "They've escaped the grasp of the underworld and get to live another day!"

Rachel's palms reconnect with the floor, chest sinking so that her shoulder blades protrude out of her black spaghetti-string top. She's hunched over the jar, over the fire, staring into it like her eyes are satisfying themselves on flame.

"I think we should put Chris's name in first," she says. There's a low growl to her voice like she's become another person. Assumed the position of the monster.

Adena's eyebrows furrow. "Chris? Why Chris? What's he ever done to you?"

Rachel cracks her neck and Adena startles.

"In second grade," Rachel starts, "I wore a skirt to school for the first time against my parents' wishes. I knew they'd yell at me when I got home but I did it anyway because I wanted to." Rachel's face sours. "And that butt-fuck, Chris Henry, made fun of my hairy legs in front of the entire class."

Adena's eyes go wide. Rachel looks so serious. But then Adena laughs, she can't help it, and then Rachel is laughing too, both of them cackling like their lungs are filled with pop rocks.

"I'm serious!" Rachel snorts. Her fingers wipe away tears—Adena has always wondered how the marker never transfers onto her face. "I was really upset! I gathered all this strength to show up in a cute skirt and Chris completely ruined it!"

"Well it's your fault for not knowing proper skirt etiquette."

Rachel sits on her calves and shoves Adena slightly. "What does that even mean?"

"Nothing. It means absolutely nothing."

They settle down and Rachel writes the name onto the corner of a notebook page which she tears off and sets aside. She rotates the notebook and slides it in front of Adena.

"Okay, your turn. Who do you pick?"

Adena worries the corner of her bottom lip between her teeth. "No one."

Rachel pouts, but her eyes say she already knows Adena is thinking of someone. That she's not as pure as she likes to seem.

"You're telling me there isn't one person in the entire world you'd like to have all-consuming power over?"

Adena's eyes flick to Rachel then back to the jar.

There is. But . . .

But it's all just fun and games, right? It's not real.

It can't be real.

"Ramon Moore."

Rachel's eyebrow cocks and her spine straightens with interest. Her tongue slips out to lick her top lip then disappears just as quickly.

But Adena saw it.

"Ramon Moore? Why Ramon Moore?"

Adena shrugs. "I mean, he was the main reason for it. It wouldn't have happened if it weren't for him."

"I'd argue it wouldn't have happened if it weren't for Bitch Three dragging you across the playground."

Ah, yes. Bitch Three; Chloe, Chanel, Christine. The three who thought it a good idea to drag Adena across the soccer field during fifth grade recess and force her to confess her feelings to Ramon Moore. Who taunted her all the painful while as everyone watched:

*"Adena wants to confess her love to you!"*

*"She like likes you, Ramon!"*

*"What are you gonna do about it? Do you like like her too?"*

*Ramon had frowned. He had the soccer ball cradled in his arm and tucked it into his stomach as he bent down to meet Adena's eye level.*

*"I'm sorry," he had said. "I like someone else."*

The wick crackles, its flame casting light over Rachel's face. She seems hesitant but then resigns.

"All right, girl. The power is in your hands so wield it as you wish."

She passes Adena a pen and Adena takes it between her fingers. It feels heavy. It feels heavy even as it spills ink along the drag of her penmanship.

But it's all a joke. It's all just a game.

She tears the piece off, Ramon's name caged within frayed edges, and together, they cast their decisions into the jar. Rachel shuts the lid and they both wait in anticipation. When the lid is removed, the names are gone, burned to ash, and the flame is extinguished.

A chill runs up Adena's spine. She looks to Rachel, to the top of Rachel's brunette head, and feels dread wash over her. Was this a bad choice? But then Rachel lifts to look at her, to meet her stare. And she's smiling.

And Adena is smiling back.

They burst into laughter. And they're on top of each other, trying to stop the other from laughing until their chests' rupture. Trying to keep quiet enough so that Rachel's mom doesn't come storming into the basement, demanding answers.

The back of Adena's head rests on Rachel's stomach. She can feel her still pulsating with giggles as they both look to the ceiling. The room smells like smoke, and the lights from the electronics blink green and blue hues. The real world is calming when you give it a chance to reach you.

It's silly, isn't it? How easily we let fantasies scare us. Because it's not real. It's never real.

And it's, oh, so fun to play games.

The following Monday at school, Ramon and Chris are absent. Adena tries to hide her look of shock as she stares at the two empty desks in Algebra 2, but she can feel the expression twisting her skin.

When she turns to Rachel standing beside her at the entrance of the class, she expects to see a mirrored expression. And she does. But only for a moment.

Rachel's shock morphs into something else. Into something hungry. She licks her lips and grins.

"What the hell?" Adena whispers.

She nudges Rachel's shoulder and Rachel snaps out of it, turning to her wide-eyed. She shrugs.

The teacher speaks up. Adena had almost forgotten where she was, and his voice startles her.

"Would you both care to join us or will you be gawking for the remainder of the period?"

Rachel and Adena clear their throats, apologize, and take their seats.

"Now, today we'll be covering parabolic formulas . . . "

Adena can't stop staring at the empty desks. They're like magnets, dragging her attention forward, pressurizing her skin.

Is it possible? Really possible?

Could they have caused this?

Without turning her eyes away, she leans toward Rachel and whispers, "Must be a coincidence, right?"

The answer is direct, sure of nothing else in the world: "I don't think so."

Adena rotates herself away from the empty desks to look at Rachel. Her friend leans back in her seat, knees propped against her desk as she stares into space, thinking. Adena watches her, watches the upturn of her lips as she chews on the end of a pencil, and wonders what could possibly be going on in that harrowing mind.

"I think we've uncovered something great," Rachel says.

Adena places her food tray on the table while Rachel opens her lunchbox. She pulls out half a sandwich, stares inside, flips the box around, and they both confirm its emptiness. Rachel sighs and grabs the bag of chips off Adena's plate.

"Hey!"

"Listen. If this is for real," Rachel says. "Like, just imagine if this is for real." She takes a bite out of her sandwich, admiring the scenery behind Adena. The plain white wall.

Because it's her thoughts that are the most colorful right now.

Adena forks her salad and rubs it around the dressing at the bottom of her plate, collecting the flavor.

"I don't think it's for real," she responds and she can feel Rachel's eyes shift to her. "And even if it is, I don't think we should mess around with it anymore."

Rachel crosses her arms and harrumphs. "That's what you think."

"Besides, Ramon and Chris are good friends. Maybe they just played hooky or they're home si—"

Something slams into Adena's back. She's shoved forward and her lungs evacuate with a grunt, ribs crushed against the edge of the table. Her plastic fork breaks against her Styrofoam plate and she struggles to keep her face from slamming into her tray as well.

There's a cackle from behind. She hears Rachel mutter the word *bitches*.

"Oh, so sorry, Adena!"

Adena recognizes that voice. Chloe.

"I didn't see you there! My bad!"

Rachel growls then barks. "The table is the size of your fat ass, Chloe, and you didn't see it?"

"I just overheard you talking about Ramon," Chloe continues, ignoring Rachel's comment.

As Adena composes herself, Chloe approaches her side. Two manicured hands press down on the table next to her and brown eyes set in a caramel frame follow. They squint into slits as Chloe twists around to assure herself in Adena's field of vision.

"You shouldn't worry about Ramon." She's so close Adena can smell the bubblegum on her hot breath. "He called me this morning and said he wasn't interested in socializing with normies today."

"What does that even mean?" Rachel says with disgust.

"He said he didn't feel like dodging any weirdo's advances. He'd rather just stay at home and play hooky."

"Do you actually believe you sound intelligent when you speak, Chloe?"

There are snickers from the other two behind; Chanel and Christine. Adena meets Chloe's stare, but she feels calm. Bitch Three's methods of intimidation have never bothered her.

All bark and no bite. Sometimes.

"You really should get Ramon out of your mind." Hot pink bubblegum. "You're a bother to him." Doesn't she get sick of chewing on that all the time? "Or do we have to teach you another lesson?"

There it is. The final move.

Adena thinks about smiling. About chuckling and patting Chloe on the head to belittle her. Tell her that's fine. She's a free woman and can do whatever she wants. Adena really couldn't care less if they dragged her through the parking lot concrete. She just wants to finish her lunch.

But she doesn't get the chance.

The chair across from her screeches against the linoleum floor. Something slams into the table, threatening destruction.

No, not something. Adena already knows.

"It's bad enough you're polluting the air, goblin. Worse that you're still here." Rachel's trying to keep her voice low. Adena can sense the struggle. She vibrates with it. If Vice Principal Merch passes by and hears Rachel's voice raised above the decibel of a blender, he'll call her into his office for a chat. It would be their third chat and it would mean suspension. "If you don't get your hands off the table, I'll remove them for you."

Chloe turns to Rachel with a wry grin. Her fingers tip-toe across the table toward her and brush the back of her hand.

"What are you gonna do, Rachel?" she mocks. "Mug me like you let your mother be mugged?"

There's a moment, a single moment where Rachel is silent. Where the air is solid and there's the possibility that Rachel decides today to be the bigger person.

Instead, she explodes.

*"No, but I'll rip your tongue out and shove it so far up your ass you'll taste how empty your skull is!"*

Adena stands, her body a piston shoving Chloe aside in the process of her ascent. Chloe snarls as she pinwheels her arms for balance. Good, let her direct her cruel energy at someone else. She doesn't realize Adena just saved her from what Rachel has no qualms of becoming.

"What gives, Adena?" Chloe yips. "You almost knocked me to the ground."

"I think that's enough, Chloe. Wouldn't you say?"

Chloe glares, fists clenched at her side. Chanel and Christine are silent, watching the scene like entertained observers.

"I've lost my appetite." Adena picks up her tray and turns from Chloe to Rachel. "Let's go."

Rachel's trembling. Her shoulders shake and Adena prays for eye contact. Prays that Rachel looks at her instead of focusing on the bullseye target she's marked on Chloe's forehead.

*C'mon. Don't let her get to you.*

Rachel screams. The length of her arm hits the table and clears it in one violent swoop. The lunchbox, half eaten sandwich, and chips clatter to the floor. The cafeteria goes silent. Heat rises to Adena's cheeks, but she forces herself to remain composed.

"I've lost my appetite too," Rachel grumbles.

"Young lady!"

*Fuck. Merch.*

Adena and Rachel spot the vice principal heading their way from across the cafeteria. Rachel grits her teeth, picks up her backpack, and storms out the doors into the hallway. Adena watches her go, but she doesn't follow. She remains in place.

Merch arrives at her side, huffing like the few feet he's covered are akin to a marathon. He takes out a handkerchief and dabs his sweaty forehead with a sigh.

"Hello, Chloe. Chanel. Christine," he says in greeting. Bitch Three chirps in feigned enthusiasm. And then he turns to her. "Miss Adena. I'd advise you to inform your friend that running away won't rid her of her problems. Next time you see Rachel, please tell her to report to my office."

Adena's eyes scan over his face. Deep-set wrinkles canyoned by sagging skin and fat. White teeth. The lack of a chin that makes his frustrations all the more comical.

Silently, she nods.

"Good," Merch confirms. "If she doesn't appear in my office by end of day tomorrow, you will be held accountable as well. Do I make myself clear?"

Another nod.

Merch straightens his wool blazer. Readjusts himself and steadies his breathing. "Ladies," he declares then saunters off.

Bitch Three cackles. This time, Chanel speaks up.

"Why are you hanging with a loser like Rachel anyway?"

"She's nothing but trouble," Christine adds.

"And she'll take you down with her."

Adena stares at Chloe. She thinks about explaining what it means to truly care about someone regardless of their misgivings. To offer kindness in the darkest of times, even when pieces of yourself are being shredded for it.

She thinks about explaining what love is.

But it would be wasted on her.

So she simply shrugs and walks away.

When she enters the hallway, she finds the corridors empty. She walks down them, searching classrooms and bathrooms. She spends the rest of the day trying to find Rachel. Trying to text her and call her but to no avail.

It's as if she's disappeared from existence.

The next day Ramon and Chris are still absent, and now, so are Rachel and Bitch Three. Adena doesn't find them at lunch and realizes that Merch isn't around either to warn her that the clock is ticking. Adena calls Rachel's cell over and over again, but there is no answer. The school is buzzing with tension; talks of missing person reports arise now that parents are unable to account for their children's whereabouts. The principal is demanding answers for their second in command's absence and teachers silence students' speculations and ghost stories about those who just *disappeared* as they scurry down the halls.

During her last class, Adena sits at her desk, staring at a blank notebook. Her fists are clenched on either side of the page and she tenses every muscle in her body wondering if she could shrink away if she tries hard enough.

She doesn't. She's still here.

There are five minutes of class remaining. Five minutes of school.

Adena picks up her pen. It feels unbearable in her hand. She brings the ballpoint to the top right-hand corner of the page and scribbles something down. When she's done, she tears the corner off from the notebook and slides the piece into her pocket.

The bell rings.

Adena stands from her desk, shrugs on her backpack, and leaves the school. In the wake of her departure, she realizes she's leaving behind an institution that will surely witness terror in the coming days.

One way or another.

Adena stands in front of Rachel's home. It's a thin thing, tilting to one side almost like it's weighed down by disappointment. The windows are dirty and the paint chipped. To most, it looks unlivable, but Adena knows better. It has its own charm. One that not many would understand.

Adena's always loved this house. Ever since she was a kid and Rachel invited her over after weeks of building trust. They'd play in the front yard because the backyard was all concrete and rust. People would pass by, stare at the two children on the lawn, then turn to the house and realize just how little is needed to live.

How resilient human survival is.

This house. Adena's always imagined this house is what Rachel looks like on the inside, that she'd be the one to fix it.

Hopefully today is that day.

Adena knocks on the front door. There is no answer.

She knocks again, this time calling out, "Hello?"

Rachel's mother must be at work. But the door is unlocked which means someone's home.

Adena pushes the door open slowly. It creaks on its hinges and she enters the foyer.

"Rachel?" she calls. But it comes out as a whisper, afraid for her presence to be known. Afraid of Rachel seeing her first.

Adena walks through the living room, through the kitchen, past the pantry and to the basement door. She reaches her hand into her pocket, worries the texture of the notebook paper between her thumb and index finger, and twists the knob.

She sneezes. The scent of burning wicks and ash tickles her nostrils. It smells like a crematorium. Like what you'd imagine school supplies would smell like if you set an office store on fire.

She descends the stairs carefully, trying not to make a sound, her heart pounding in her chest like a convict begging for freedom, but she already knows Rachel can hear her. She knew of her presence the moment she stepped through the front door.

"I've spent enough time in this house to know what every room sounds like from the basement," Rachel had bragged to her once. "It's like I'm the brain of the house and I can hear all the parts and their happenings . . . Not that there's much happening anymore anyway."

Adena reaches the final step. She sees the jar before she sees Rachel. It's five feet away from her, lit with scraps of paper littered about it like discarded confetti. Rachel sits beyond it, far enough that the light doesn't reach her. Far enough that she's in the dark.

"Rachel?" Adena steps forward, then stops when Rachel's head lifts to meet her. The flickering glow shines off her eyes. Black eyes filled with pain and hellfire.

"I never told you this," Rachel starts so abruptly. The crackle of the wick, hungry and waiting, fills the silence between her words. "But after my mom got mugged . . . I researched endlessly to find the names of the guys who did it. Three of them." Rachel reveals her hand in the corona of light. Between her fingers are three pieces of paper. "I got lucky, really. It was only because they got caught in a later robbery that I was able to connect the dots." Rachel laughs a hateful laugh, her teeth shining like individual pearls through the dark. "The robbery got newspaper coverage. Three goons walk into a deli, three goons walk out in handcuffs. No injuries, no stolen property. No harm, no foul. Just good ol' journalism."

Adena takes another step forward. "Rachel . . . " She reaches out, thin fingers casting spider-like silhouettes across the walls, trying to connect the distance between them.

"Do you know my mom can barely stand to look at me?" Rachel snaps. She leans in and the creases of her face are caught by shadows. "Looking at me reminds her of that night." She looks monstrous. "Like I'm the reason those guys came after her." Rachel screams, "*I was only ten!* What could I have possibly done?"

Rachel's hand turns into a fist, taking the papers along with it. And then her fingers open, one by one above the jar, until the fist is a palm ready to deliver a slap and the papers fall to their fiery deaths below.

The jar glows bright as it consumes the names.

"But it's not just them who have to pay," Rachel mutters. She's tearing pieces from her notebook, curled over her work like a predator protecting their hunt. "How about my mom's boss who made her work a double shift? Who made her stay late to bag groceries while he sat in the back office smoking a joint? How about the Wilkes who passed by the alley, who made fucking eye contact with a terrified girl who didn't know what to do to protect her mother and walked away? Or the cop, too lazy and too stupid to do any real investigating." She's scribbling names across the ripped pages, frantic like if she doesn't do so fast enough, her opportunity will vanish out of existence.

"Rachel . . . " Adena tries again. She doesn't want to ask, but she has to know. "Did you put Chloe, Chanel, and Christine's names in the jar?"

Rachel's head snaps up. Her upper lip curls over her teeth in a snarl.

"Oh, don't do that," she says. "Don't use their names like they're people. We've always called them Bitch Three and now you want to double back and humanize them?"

Adena takes another step forward. She's standing above Rachel now, reading the names on all those papers.

Arnold Holtz.

Stephanie Wilkes.

Charles Wilkes.

Detective Go Fuck Yourself.

"I tried to group them." Rachel giggles a crazed giggle like a scientist realizing the true extent of their creation. "I wrote a few test names on a piece of paper and burned them. People that won't be missed. But it's too early to know how it all works. I think it comes for them at night. I think it comes and it just takes them and then the next day they're just gone. Not a trace. Can you believe that?"

Rachel picks up the pieces. She holds them over the fire.

*Innocent people,* Adena thinks. *Innocent people who just so happened to be involved in a horrific night.*

"Are they really so innocent though?" Rachel says.

Adena's skin floods with goosebumps. Over the soft flesh of Rachel's bottom lip seeps a trickle of saliva. Her black eyes glitter, whites drowning in darkness until there's no presence of humanity left.

Rachel's voice declares in a hoarse echo, "I'm going to be a fucking god."

Adena screams and the sound catches Rachel off guard, her eyes returning to the mortal present and looking to Adena for an explanation. But Adena has already made her leap. She jumps over the jar and tackles Rachel to the ground, gripping her wrist and slamming it into the floor in hopes of forcing her to release the names. But Rachel is stronger. Standing five inches taller than Adena and fighting off demons for a living, Rachel overpowers her easily.

There's a grunt, a rip, and Rachel rolls Adena over to claim the higher ground.

Adena shrieks. Rachel foams at the mouth.

"I can't let you—" *do this*, Adena attempts, but she's silenced by a fist to the face. Her brain scrambles in her head, registering the sensation of knuckles cracking against her nose while commanding her lungs not to inhale her own blood. Rachel crawls off her and Adena cries, taking air in through her mouth with rasping breaths now that her nose has been decommissioned.

"Rachel," she weeps.

But Rachel doesn't reply. She doesn't need to. When Adena peers over her chest, she witnesses Rachel drop the names into the jar. She witnesses the hungry glow like a furnace gratified for the wood chips that keep it alive.

"I learned that night," Rachel says, staring into the fire, "that if you show you're weak, people will take advantage of you. If you let them, they'll do it without thinking twice."

Adena turns over. She crawls on her forearms to Rachel's backside. She keeps her body moving although her heart is begging her to stop. Pleading. Tears trail down her face. *I thought I could fix her*, she thinks. *I thought I could tilt her upright and paint her beautiful and safe.* Adena reaches into her pocket and pulls out the torn paper.

*I thought I could fix her . . .*

With a whimper, Adena reaches past Rachel and lets her fingers open up like a dying flower shriveling wide to let Death in. From her fingertips falls Rachel's name, falling and falling until it hits the lip of the jar. There it pauses, undecided. Adena holds her breath as the piece teeters.

Rachel makes her move. Adena reaches out to stop her but doesn't get there in time.

Rachel bends.

She blows.

The name falls into the depths of the ceramic and burns up. Adena's shout catches in her throat, a sob ramming through the organ's walls at the same time, multiple emotions blocking the exit.

*Why?* she wants to ask.

"It wouldn't be fair, would it," Rachel answers, "if I didn't wager my own death. After all, I'm the one who let it happen. I was the weak one."

*How silly . . .*

"Then again, I am the one who created this jar." Rachel tilts her head back and stares up at the ceiling, contemplating. "And can a cursed object really destroy another cursed object?" A pause. "I guess we'll see."

*I could never fix her. How could I fix something that's already demolished?*

Adena's eyes grow wide watching Rachel's hand lift into her field of vision, a piece of paper larger than a fist wedged between those decorated fingers.

A piece of paper with her name on it.

"I knew you'd try to take me down," Rachel says.

"I—"

When Adena tries to speak, blood falls into her mouth, onto her tongue. She's assaulted by the taste and snaps her jaws tight.

"*I had to,*" Rachel finishes the thought for her. "Yes, I know, I know. So I hope you understand why *I* have to."

Rachel releases her fingers. The piece falls. It burns. A sharp pang hits Adena's chest at the scent of her name turned to ashes. She falls too. Collapses in defeat. The air . . . She becomes drowsy. The air becomes a suppressant. A gas.

She can barely hear Rachel speak.

"You always protected me. Against Bitch Three and Merch." Whispers. "But the real question is why . . ."

Adena's eyes are winking. Slowly, slowly shutting.

"I was the weak one. But you kept me weak."

The air is turning grey. They're in a crematorium. There are bodies burning everywhere.

"I won't let you . . ."

Adena doesn't register unconsciousness but she falls just the same.

When Adena comes to, she is still on Rachel's basement floor. The room is dark. The jar is in the same place, only the light is snuffed from inside. The scent of smoke still lingers in the air, only it's not as pungent as before.

Adena sits up. She licks her lips and her tongue runs across crust. She remembers the nosebleed. She touches her fingers to her bridge to check how much she's bled out. If maybe she's close to exsanguination. Her fingers last no longer than half a second upon the cartilage. The pain is too excruciating.

Broken. It's definitely broken.

She sets her hands back behind her, propping her upper body against her arms. She scans the room.

The basement looks empty. But it doesn't feel empty.

Something rustles in the corner. Adena turns to it, eyes wide, trying to collect what light she can to see in the dark. But it's no use. Her senses only pick up sound. The rustling grows louder, more confident. It doesn't care that someone else is here to observe its presence. It wants to be known.

Adena crawls backward, arms and legs working to drag her bottom across the carpet. As she moves, her hand hits something that creates a clatter like soft rain.

The matches.

The rustling stops, sensing her activity. Adena holds her breath. Stares through the darkness, trying to imagine what could be here with her.

And then the rustling moves. More like a shifting weight than the sound of a small rat searching for food, the rustle approaches her direction. Adena's heart races and she scrambles backward, hoping to escape its trajectory.

Her back hits something. The bottom of the staircase. Light shines down from the open door above. She leverages herself onto her arms to turn and run up the stairs, but before she can, the rustling lunges out of the darkness and pins her down.

No, not a rustling.

It's Rachel.

Rachel with black eyes and smiling lips coiling herself around her like a snake. Rachel glowing like a ghost, her skin luminescent and throat purring like a lullaby. She doesn't say a word. Her hand caresses Adena's cheek lovingly. So cold. Her skin is so cold. But her gaze is hot, filled with hunger. Her legs straddle Adena's waist as she leans in. There is no pulse to her contact. No affection. Only motion.

"You knew," Adena finds herself saying. "You knew this whole time, didn't you?"

Rachel doesn't speak, but she listens. Adena knows she's listening somewhere deep down in that possessed mind of hers. Veins grow on her face and her lips abandon their pinkish color for a grey hue.

And still, from the way Rachel is watching her as she descends chest to chest, Adena knows part of this is real.

Heat surges through Adena. A twisted anger feeding off a perverted release. How funny. How wrong. How not like she ever imagined. And this is on purpose, isn't it? A payback. A payback for her crimes.

"You know why I picked Ramon Moore, Rachel?" Adena snarls. "You want me to admit it?" She wants to scream. She wants to scream it so loud it breaks Rachel's eardrums. But she keeps her voice down. If this is her final confession, she needs to deliver it well. "After Bitch Three finished their public humiliation of me . . . "

Adena sees it. She sees it like it's right in front of her. She sees herself in the hallways of their elementary school searching for Rachel. Running down the corridors of chipped eggshell white walls and rotten orange juice tiles. She sees herself turning that final corner and sees Rachel with Ramon. Rachel hugging Ramon. Ramon kissing Rachel with the inexperience of a child still in size junior shoes.

She sees herself retreat. She feels her jealousy. It's steam. The kind so hot it burns layers deep.

"I didn't want Ramon."

She sees Ramon's eyes lowering to meet hers. She sees his lips move with words she couldn't care less for.

"I realized I wanted you. And that was even more humiliating."

Rachel smiles. It's weak, but it shows she understands. Even if this is a lost part of Rachel. An antithesis.

"I picked Ramon," Adena says. This is her confession. This is her confession for the sin that has cursed her. "I picked Ramon because he got from you what I wanted."

The admission is awful. It's selfish and predatory. It's resentment, a curse Adena has always hated from herself. But it's real. And still, Rachel leans in. Her hip bones dig into the small of Adena's stomach and Adena realizes this is her chance. Her chance to have what she's wanted for so long.

Rachel's lips approach, harsh grey things with intent. Adena puckers hers, waiting for the taste. But the flavor never comes. She gasps. She screams. She tries to sit up, but Rachel won't let her. No, not Rachel. A mirror. A reflection. It's no longer black eyes belonging to her friend that bore down on her. It's her own. She's screaming. The doppelganger is screaming. Her hands are around her neck, choking the life out of her. This is Adena's antithesis. Her shadow self.

Her cursed object.

And as this jealousy, this rage, this pent-up resentment slides down her throat like black tar, and as her esophagus and stomach fill with the saccharine sludge, she realizes she was cursed far before a jar could tell her otherwise.

The jar fills with dark oil. It zaps the energy from the room, consuming it like a treat. Rachel reaches under the couch and pulls out the lid from where it was kicked. She stares into the dark reflective surface and grins.

"There you are."

She caps the jar with the lid. It makes a satisfying click, rubber vacuuming ash and smoke into a black hole.

"I knew you'd never hurt me," she purrs.

There are thumps from upstairs. Footsteps. It's Rachel's mother returning home and approaching the basement door. Probably wondering what's going on. But she won't open it. Rachel knows this. She'll only get so far until her threshold of care reaches its limit. She'll place her hand on the doorknob. She'll think. She'll hesitate.

The footsteps retreat. Rachel scans the ceiling, marking the path her mother takes. A path that leads far away from her.

That's all right. Not a worry. After all, the strongest work in the dark. Under the radar of those they are affecting.

Rachel reaches for her notebook.

That's all right.

She opens to a fresh new page and grips the pen within her claw.

That's just fine.

She scratches at the scales on her arm. Runs the fork of her tongue across the fangs in her maw.

It's no matter.

She whips her tail against the carpet to mimic the heartbeat she no longer has.

She has much to do. She can't be distracted, anyhow.

She scans the page, then begins writing, monstrous eyes hungry for a list of sinners.

The list is endless.

Good.

Cursed objects are not limited by time. And neither is Rachel's hunger.

# THE STONE

JOSEPH SALE

BUT CHRIST, it was a fucking big toad. It squatted in the sere gorse sprouting from the clifftop like the last few desperate remnants of hair on a balding man's pate. The toad's flesh was shiny and multicoloured, as though it'd been baptised in petrol. The benevolent look on its face didn't quite detract from how slimy it was.

The toad was maybe just larger than a football, freakishly big. Cassandra couldn't take her eyes off it, but she was also a good deal repulsed. Mark stood behind her with shameless cowardice, so goggle-eyed it was comic.

"Do you think it's radioactive?" he whispered, as though worried the toad might hear and take offence. "I'm getting distinct Godzilla vibes."

"Well, it's almost certainly poisonous. I wouldn't touch it for a million quid."

The toad let out a deep-throated croak. It sounded vaguely like approval. That done, it hopped away from them in a lumbering motion, moving deeper into the gorse.

"What the hell is it doing here?" Mark asked.

Cassandra was wondering the same thing. The cliffs overlooking Bournemouth beach were certainly a place of natural beauty: the dense briar formed a tangled forest for tiny mammals to scurry through, and even one or two goats. Below them golden sand met waves redolent of the Mediterranean on a good day: turquoise greens and blues, crystalline sapphire, and occasionally deep emerald. The horizon was a vagueness where sky and sea seemed to meet and become one. But, for all this, it wasn't the place one expected to find a toad. They weren't saltwater creatures. And the cliffs were miles from the nearest pond or lake.

"It's left something," Cassandra said.

There was a gleaming object where the toad had previously sat.

"Probably a shit, dear."

"No, no, it's glowing . . . "

"Radioactive shit?"

Cassandra gave him a "shut up" look and he obliged. She stepped off the clifftop path and waded through nettles and sharp branches to reach the spot where the toad had been sitting.

Nestled in the bright gorse and tricksy thorns was what looked like a lump of meteorite.

Its surface was rough, knobbly and greenish, a little like the toad itself. The rock, for that's what it surely had to be, was perhaps the size of a beer can. There was a hole in either end.

The longer she looked, the more she saw. There were faint green veins coursing through the rock. If she squinted, the whole object seemed to emit a charged light, similar to the colours that smeared across the eyelid when she shut her eyes.

The cliffs were pale sandstone, and the quarries near Dorset were limestone; this certainly could not have come from around Bournemouth. It closely resembled an onyx gemstone, but the more she thought about it, the more she believed her original hypothesis was likely the most accurate: this was a meteor, and a fucking big one.

Without thinking, she reached out and grabbed it.

"Cassandra!"

The stone was shockingly cold to the touch, which she had not expected. As she wrapped her fingers around it, the luminous colours shone through the flesh of her hand.

"You're nuts," Mark said, faintly.

She rounded on him.

"This could be worth something." She had no intention of selling it, however.

"I thought you said you wouldn't touch it for a million quid?"

"That was the toad."

She traipsed back to him through the undergrowth, a little guiltily, pocketing the stone or meteor or whatever it was in her coat.

Mark put his arm around her, a conciliatory gesture, and the two walked on, continuing their usual route.

They took a zig-zagging path at Portman's Ravine down to the beach. They strolled along, smiling at dog walkers. Eventually, both caved and bought an ice cream: Mark a Magnum, and Cassandra a 99 Flake (they both moaned about how they were no longer 99p—the greatest marketing scam of the century). As the sun began to set behind the cliffs, lengthening the shadows over the water, they decided to call it a day. They bid farewell to the sea, which sighed in response, the sound of its tide soporific and melancholy. Yes, they had to go now or they'd end up kipping on the beach. Time was forever running out on these perfect moments.

They took the path back up Portman's Ravine and along the cliffs to their car. They lived on the other side of the city, and it would only be a fifteen-minute drive home. Unfortunately, a lot could happen in fifteen minutes; worlds could fall and cultures could change.

They took this walk so regularly, and everything was so familiar—barring the toad and its stone—that Mark did not twig to the other car which had pulled out of the lot just after him. He didn't mark the three young men with resolute insanity on their faces. He didn't realise he was being tailed. Cassandra saw even less. She was inspecting the meteor in her hands, turning it over and feeling its ridges and seams—it was like reading braille. Its most defining feature was the circular hole that bore through its full width.

The big question she was now trying to answer was why did it have the hole? The rational answer was water-erosion, but the meteor was surely too big to have a perfect cylinder eroded through it lengthways. No. Someone had made the hole, which meant this wasn't a random hunk of rock that'd fallen from the sky, but a tool or instrument of some kind.

"I think aliens made this, Mark," she said, though not without humour.

Mark gave her a nervous sideways glance.

"Then should we be taking it home?"

"You worried about getting anal probed?"

"Always, Cass. Always."

"If anything bad happens, we'll go back there and throw it into the sea."

She knew she was lying even as she spoke, but she wasn't sure why the meteor had become so important to her. Maybe it was simply because it was the first time anything otherworldly or out of the ordinary had happened in her life. She worked in a marketing firm as a graphic designer, and had steadily climbed the ranks to team-lead. She'd married Mark pretty young. He was every bit the eligible candidate, an accountant with solid income and good prospects. Now they had started a mortgage on their first house, they were talking about children every other day. Her life was unfolding according to society's edicts with almost textbook orthodoxy.

And somewhere deep down it rankled.

The reason she had become a graphic designer was not because she wanted to have a stable job or work in marketing. It was only supposed to be a temporary thing on her path to becoming a digital fantasy artist. As a kid, the insane, psychedelic covers of *Make Your Myth* books by John Grant had blown her mind. That's what she'd wanted to do: make images that transported the viewer to other worlds.

But somehow, mundane life had snared her. She was in its hold, and it didn't want to let her go. Her only tie to her past self, a self in love—nay, worshipful—of the fantastic, was Mark's nerdiness. She was so grateful for him in that moment she could have cried.

"You okay?" he said.

Damn him for being so sensitive.

"Yeah," she replied. "Weird, but this has got me thinking about a whole bunch of things."

Mark nodded, as if this were perfectly reasonable.

They pulled into the driveway and Cassandra experienced something like relief as she put away the stone again.

"Netflix and chill?" he asked, putting a gentle, warm hand on her thigh.

He knew just how to cheer her up.

As Cassandra turned to the door, she sensed something was wrong. She could hear voices nearby, down the street.

"Just fuckin' waste 'em."

Her blood ran cold and suddenly the car—a metal protective shell—seemed the safest place to be; she withdrew her hand from the door-handle. This was a folly. She was no safer in than out. In fact, she was trapped.

"What the—?" Mark began.

Two young men appeared at his side of the car, and one in front of Cassandra. The chill that'd ran through her now became more of a paralysing venom. Her breaths squeezed out and in through clenched teeth. Her heart pounded.

There was a glint in the night, something metal.

A gun.

"Fuckin' do 'em, Aidy!"

The gunshot, followed by shattering glass, was the loudest sound she had ever heard. Once. Twice. She turned and saw Mark foaming at the mouth, blood soaking his shirt and splashed across the wheel, two bullet holes in his chest.

"Do 'em both!"

She didn't have time to scream as the third shot sent pain exploding through her belly. She uttered a kind of gargling sound as she attempted to shriek and blood filled her mouth.

"Go! Go!" one of the men urged.

They fled like shades into the night. Just before she heard a car door opening, one of them said, "You're in, Aidy. You've earned your stripes, mate."

An engine roared, and the car sped away without headlights.

She tried to wail, to scream. She touched her stomach, where the grisly puncture wound leaked crimson all over her jeans and the faux-leather seat. The pain was unbelievable, but the fear was greater; she was going to die, and Mark, Mark . . . No, he couldn't be dead.

She reached over, hands smeared and ghastly. She felt at his neck for a pulse. He did not stir at her touch. He was frighteningly still, like a crash test dummy.

"Mark . . . "

She called to him, but there was no response. Tears burned her eyes. What she felt now was a deeper pain than the bullet wound. That was a local pain, a pinprick of intensity that made her want to vomit; the grief, on the other hand, enveloped all of her like a dark, merciless sea.

Mark had no pulse. There was no life in Mark's still-open and glassy eyes. A bullet had gone through his heart.

Cassandra sobbed. She screamed at the senseless cruelty of it.

Through her maelstrom of pain, a quiet voice spoke.

*Get it together. You have to do something.*

Yes, call an ambulance. She'd read somewhere you could live for a long time with a stomach wound. She could yet survive . . .

A darker voice answered the first.

*But what's the point in that?*

Everything she had lived for lay dead next to her. And those men . . . she shook with agonising rage. What she wouldn't do to get them. Kill them, even. Her whole life she had been a gentle soul, but now some terror had been awoken in her that longed for vengeance of the most despicable and bloody kind.

But what could she tell the police? She'd seen no license plate, not even the make of the car. If she was honest with herself, she could not even recall the men's faces, it'd happened so fast, and they had been hooded and masked.

The tears came anew, each one like extracting a bullet.

She searched her coat pocket for a tissue with the absurd notion of stymying the flow of blood. Her fingers found the stone. She took it out and regarded it. In the midst of her suffering the object only seemed to hold greater fascination. She thought she could see green flames licking from its surface, but perhaps that was just blood loss. Her bloodied hands left it wetted. It shone dire and true in this, her darkest night.

Suddenly, she knew what she had to attempt. Maybe it would be the last thing she ever did, but it was now the only path available to her. Her life had taken a strange deviation from the comfort of the norm, and now she had to answer in kind.

With Herculean effort, she forced open the car door. She staggered out into the freezing night air. Lurching like a zombie, she made her way around the car over to Mark's side. She pulled open the door.

She bit her lip, drew in a deep, painful breath. She undid Mark's seatbelt and pulled. He was tougher to shift than she thought, but eventually he tumbled out of the driver's seat and into their driveway, an ignorable heap.

"I'm sorry, my love."

The pain in her belly was an ocean current, inescapable and dragging her down; she had undoubtedly torn something as she wrenched Mark out of the car.

Lifting one leg into the car was a challenge. She had to hold onto the hand-straps above the door and slide herself into the vehicle like an old woman. The seat was wet with Mark's blood and her own. She pulled the door shut. She was in. A miracle.

She lay the stone on her lap.

It was only a fifteen-minute drive. She had just enough strength.

The sky was black and almost starless as she pulled into the small parking lot abutting the cliffs. The only exception was the Dog Star, Sirius, which shone like a ghastly beacon, guiding Cassandra to what she knew would be her grave.

She staggered out of the car and slammed the door shut; it reverberated in the dead silence with the ominous rumble of a toad's croak.

Silent? How ridiculous to think it. The gush and hiss of the sea below was a constant sound, an inescapable roil.

Her life was out of control, and so now the only thing left to do was submit. How often had she and Mark come to the coast to walk? It had been their Sunday morning service, their worship. How fitting her pilgrimage ended here, as foretold by the star-toad.

She stumbled across the road, over a grassy knoll, and towards the uprising of briar that marked the cliff's perilous edge. Anyone watching from one of the million-pound houses overlooking the bluffs would have thought she was blind drunk. They might have even mistaken the dark stone clutched tightly in her hands as a bottle.

Through the sharp tangles—for what did she care about a few cuts now?—until she reached the very end. Below her, around two-hundred feet, sand reached out to touch a void. The black waters rolled in like an army. The Dog-Star was twinned in the waters with its counterpart above, glaring down from the heavens in judgement.

Sea air whipped her face, filled her lungs. One step and it would all be over. The gulls would pick her clean.

But one more thing she must do first.

She drew up the bloodied stone—which was no stone but a horn—and blew. The sound it made was not of this Earth, a cosmic wailing that seemed at once like the sonorous speech of cetaceans in the deepest abyss, and the sharp keening of birds of the high arctic.

A wind struck the clifftops, nearly destabilising Cassandra, but she dropped to all fours, planting her hands, a posture of obeisance. The wind carried with it not just the tang of saltwater, but something else, a smell of sweet voids.

As she breathed raggedly through the pain, it took her a moment to realise what had occurred.

The sea had stopped.

The tide was halted, as though Time had been arrested. The waters were as glacial and motionless as a windless lake, stretching to black infinity. Yet the wind was now picking up force, battering the cliffs with potent gusts. There was some kind of red mist in the wind.

Not mist, *sand.*

Sand soaked in . . . blood?

She knew, though not sure how, that this was not sand from the beach below, but from some other realm more strange than any she could imagine; more strange than the covers of her beloved *Make Your Myth* stories. A laugh came to her then as the wind blasted with shocking power, sweeping gorse and weed flat in humility. Cassandra shielded her face with bloodied hands against the grit blowing in from another universe. Before her eyes, her hands were changing . . .

Below, the sea was stirring again. Not with the tide, but with forms. Black and hunched, pelagic and eyeless, they rose from the dark sea in ranks as numberless as the banished stars. After them came greater shapes, living cities hobbling on crustaceous legs; hidden continents returning from the deep to wage undying war. She had summoned them. For vengeance. But more than that, for *change.*

Beyond these titans was something greater by far, a secret glimpsed only by the few: at the place where she had always fantasised sea and sky met, there *was* a meeting point, a black line that seemed like a stitch, uniting every element, every force, and every dimension both seen and unseen. That stitch seemed to grow as she focused on it, no longer minute, but towering above comprehension.

The black line looked like a toad's vertical pupil. She tried to laugh again at the comparison, but this time her throat failed. A guttural croak caused her to look around. They were here, a host of toads, all of them as grotesquely large as the one she had found earlier that day, a lifetime ago. There were tens—no, hundreds—and all of them stared with single-minded concentration upon the black sigil at the end of all reality, growing larger as its armies marched up the shores. The myriad yellow eyes were each imprinted with a Tower of their own.

Cassandra tried to speak, but she could not. Her pain was gone. She was no longer Cassandra. Her flesh shone with oily luminescence. Her webbed feet were firm and unshaking. She, too, was a star-toad, one of the thousands now gathered in the cliffs.

Witness to the end of Time.

# EVERY BREATH IS A CHOICE

## MAX BOOTH III

SOMETIMES TOM PULLS his tie so tight he can't breathe, and he refuses to let go, even when the world around him begins to dissolve and his vision introduces black dots like cigarette burns on a film reel. He tells himself he'll keep pulling until the oxygen has fled his lungs, until his heart's thrown in the towel and collapsed, and sometimes he even gets close. He can feel the reaper's hand on his shoulder and he knows any second now it'll all be over, but he can't quite make it, something always makes him let go of the tie. Thoughts of Diana, maybe. Fantasies that she'll move back into the house, the house they shared together for ten years.

Ten years.

You can't forget time. You can't block a decade from your memory. They'd had good days. They'd been in love. But only he seems to remember that now. Diana's memory's topsy-turvy. Diana only remembers David. Tom remembers David, too, although he tries his best to forget.

Tom straightens his tie and goes to work. On the train, he stares out the window and fantasizes about being anybody else in this city but himself. He wonders if any of them have had to make the type of choices he's made. If any of them understand true pain. True horror. Then he fantasizes about bashing his head into the window, over and over, until the glass shatters and impales his skull.

"Tom, you look unhealthy," his coworkers say when he's roaming around the office.

"Tom, when was the last time you slept?"

"Tom, are you eating okay?"

"Tom, you look like shit."

And Tom says the same thing each time, smiling sadly, staring into a cup of cold coffee:

"Sorry."

"Sorry."

"Sorry."
"Sorry."
Always apologizing, but none of them know what for. Tom knows. Diana knows. Somewhere, David knows, too. And that's all that matters. He's sorry. So fucking sorry he can't stand it anymore. In his cubicle, he hides and calls Diana. The ring lasts as long as a penny falling into hell. She won't talk to him anymore. Won't even acknowledge he exists. It doesn't stop him from calling her every day, every hour, every heartbeat, hoping she changes her mind, hoping she decides to love him again.

It's been five years since she moved out. Five years since Victor Waterman entered their lives, and five years since David left.

The last time Tom saw Victor, the judge was sentencing the monster to life imprisonment, with no chance for parole. Tom sat in the stands, listening to the audience around him applaud, listening to Victor scream obscenities, and realized it wasn't enough. It would never be enough.

During his lunch break, Tom stands on the edge of the roof, staring at the traffic moving below like ants. He debates stepping forward and seeing if his body flies or falls. A part of him's convinced he'll just float, stagnant. This is all a dream, he's been asleep for the last five years and this is what it'll take to finally wake.

He takes out his cell phone again and calls Diana. Straight to voicemail. He speaks into the recording, tells her their lives aren't over, there's still time to make things work. Tells her he's still the man she fell in love with.

Although sometimes he has trouble deciding which is stronger, his love for Diana or his hate for Victor.

Maybe they're the same thing.

The first time Tom saw Victor was a Saturday. The fact that it's a Saturday sticks out clearly, because Tom never worked on Saturdays. But that week, Stuart Jackson called in sick at the office, so Tom wasn't given a choice. He had to cancel his plans to take David to the park, even though he'd specifically *promised* him they'd play basketball that afternoon. Tom hated breaking promises to his son. Hated that look of disappointment, of distrust. It's one of the few faces Tom can remember of his son these days. He tries to remember what his smile looked like, but every time he thinks about it, all he sees is a distorted orb, a universe of blood where his mouth should be, a sea of tears and screams begging for help, for his daddy to save him.

That's what daddies are for, after all. Saving their sons. Making sure no harm comes their way.

Bad daddy, bad daddy, bad, bad, bad.

The first time he saw Victor, the monster had been stepping out of Tom's bathroom. Diana was on the ground with blood leaking down her thighs and David was tied to the radiator across the room. Both their mouths were duct-taped. Victor exited the bathroom, walked into the bedroom and caught Tom standing there, staring at the scene, not understanding any of it. Then Victor reached on top of Tom's nightstand, picked up a gun that Tom'd never seen before, and pointed it at Diana.

After Tom's lunch break is over, he returns to his cubicle. Coworkers are talking about last night's football game. They ask him if he watched it and he shakes his head. He doesn't even know who's in the playoffs this year, or, for that matter, who's won the last five Super Bowls. He has to be honest. None of it matters anymore. That's the thing nobody at this office can understand. Nobody here understands loss. Nobody here knows what Tom has gone through, what he's sacrificed. They're all still protected safely inside their little bubbles. Sometimes Tom imagines coming in with a knife and popping all of them, one-by-one. *This is what life is,* he would scream. This is what you've been missing.

He sits down in his chair. He stares at a computer screen. On his desk, there's photos of Diana and David. These photos are the only way he passes the time.

He wonders how Victor passes the time, if he's allowed photographs in his cell, or if he has to stare at his cock for entertainment.

When Victor walked out of the bathroom, fumbling for the pistol on the nightstand, his pants were still unzipped, cock hanging out like a defeated python covered in blood. The sight of it froze Tom, made the realization of what was happening sink in.

Then Victor pressed the gun against Diana's skull, smiling, licking his lips, looking at Tom like he was nothing.

After work, Tom drives straight home. He sits in the living room, in the middle of the sofa, imagining Diana on one side and David on the other. He opens his arms, hoping he'll feel their bodies, but only their ghosts welcome his embrace. He would cry if there were still tears left to produce, but his soul hollowed out long ago.

For dinner, he eats two slices of toast. He pours a pot of coffee down his throat because being asleep is worse than being awake. He stays up until three in the morning watching television, not hearing what anyone's saying.

Tomorrow's getting closer and he can't avoid it. The five-year anniversary. He tries to push it away, like seaweed in the ocean, but it's too late, it's stuck to his skin, clinging to his flesh, eating at him.

Tomorrow, tomorrow.

Tomorrow.

Five years ago tomorrow, Tom stood in the bedroom, shaking, staring at his bloodied wife, his terrified son. "Please," he whispered, "please don't."

"Please don't what," the man named Victor said, although Tom did not know his name yet.

"Please don't hurt them."

"I think it's too late for that."

"No. No. No."

"Yes."

Tom had never met Victor before. No one in his family had ever seen him until that Saturday. Later, Victor would admit that it was simply the first house to let him inside. He'd tried others, giving them that classic "I've broken down and need to use your phone" line, but nobody was dumb enough to buy it.

In court, Victor turned to Tom and grinned before saying, "Nobody until her."

Tom lost it. He wanted blood. But even blood-for-blood would not be enough to quench his hunger. Five years he's fantasized about getting revenge, about cutting Victor open and wearing his flesh, if just for a moment, only to feel what it was like to be a monster.

Monster, monster, monster.

On the fifth anniversary of David's death, Tom calls in from work. Instead of dialing Diana, he drives across the city to her parents' house, where she's been living the last half decade. Her father, well into his seventies, gives Tom one look and tells him to get off his property.

"You're no longer welcomed here," he says.

"I just want to see Diana."

"Well, she don't want to see you, so beat it."

"Just one minute. Please. Not today."

"I'm going to close the door now," her father says, "and if you're still out here when I reopen it, I'm gonna do what I should've done fifteen years ago before you ever married my daughter and introduce you to my sawed-off."

He closes the door.

Tom returns to his car, crying, sobbing, clawing at the steering wheel as he drives away into the fog. He is always driving into fog.

All he wants is his family back.

"Who are you?" Tom asked Victor, unable to take his eyes off the gun, off Diana's face as she silently screamed through duct tape.

"Me?" Victor said. "I'm nobody. I'm unimportant."

"Then please don't do this."

"It's already done, friend."

"Why?"

"Maybe this is punishment."

Tom fell to his knees, digging his nails into the carpet. It was all he could do to prevent his body from flinging forward and causing the gun to go off. "Punishment for what? *Punishment for what?*"

The man with the gun paused for a moment and shrugged. "I don't know. Punishment for not looking after this sweet piece of ass? Punishment for being born? Not everything has a reason, you know. Not everything needs to make sense."

"What?"

"Look, it doesn't matter. What's done is done. Now what happens next, that's what we need to discuss."

Tom trembled. "You raped my wife."

Victor nodded.

"You fucking piece of shit."

"I am."

"I'll kill you."

"We'll see."

Victor raised the gun and shot Tom in the chest. He flew onto his back, skull bouncing against the floor. Diana screamed through the duct tape. David cried for a guardian angel who never received an invitation.

In the car, Tom listens to the local conspiracy theorist on the radio rant about black helicopters and 9/11 cover-ups. Years ago, he'd have laughed at the kind of lunacy. Now, on the other hand, it sort of makes sense. Maybe the government is hiding things from them. Maybe they know what makes a monster a monster. Maybe nothing is as it seems.

He pulls into a gas station for a pack of cigarettes. A boy who barely looks old enough to drive takes his money. The boy could be anybody's son. He could be Tom's David.

Except this boy behind the counter, he ain't dead.

It was after the letters began arriving that Tom realized their marriage was doomed. Maybe it'd been doomed as soon as that last breath left their son. But Tom had managed to stay delusional until the letters started coming in. The letters from Victor. He'd missed the first couple. Diana had been hiding them, burning them, whatever, before Tom had a chance to see them. But one day he came home early, happened to stop and get the mail. Normally it wasn't his business to open his wife's letters, but he decided to make it his business once she started receiving postage with a penitentiary as the sender's address.

The first few sentences in the letter threatened Diana harm if she continued to ignore his letters. The rest of the message consisted of him professing his love to her.

Victor. In love with Diana.

Tom's wife.

Victor.

Their son's executioner.

In his rage, he'd ignored the early comments in the letter pertaining to Diana ignoring Victor. Just the fact alone that she'd been hiding the letters from Tom had been enough to raise suspicion. He'd started breaking things, hitting the bottle hard, playing Russian roulette with him and David's cat.

Eventually the cat lost.

Diana didn't sleep another night in that house. Still hasn't.

The letters continued to arrive. Tom read them all.

The motherfucker was head-over-heels.

Tom didn't know how Victor had found out he'd impregnated Diana. Maybe Diana told him, then freaked out, decided never to contact him again. But it didn't matter. The damage was done. Victor knew he now had a son.

Take one out of the world, bring another in.

Tom told her he didn't even want to know the kid's name.

"That doesn't belong to me," he'd said.

"He should've taken you instead," she'd said back.

"That wasn't an option."

Tom drives to the preschool, parks where he has a clear view of the playground. He lights up a cigarette, sits and waits. Eventually the kiddos pile out of the building and embrace the slides and swings like reunited lovers. He watches them, wondering which one is the spawn of his wife and his wife's monster.

They all look the same.

They all look like David.

They all look like corpses.

Eventually he finds the boy. He doesn't know his name, but he's seen photographs on the few occasions he was crazy enough to push past Diana's father and enter the house. Tom gets out of the car and approaches the fence. He raises his camera and snaps a few pictures, then returns to the car and drives away.

He has work to do.

The last night Tom and Diana and David were together as a happy family was the Friday before Victor introduced himself to their lives. They'd gotten a pizza and rented a movie from Blockbuster. David was thrilled because the next day they were going to play basketball at the park. Basketball was his favorite thing in the world. Pizza was his second favorite. Tom remembered clearly how David was insistent he take off all the toppings from his slice, even the cheese. It didn't matter that David could eat a pound of cheese by itself—just not on pizza.

"No toppings, Daddy. That's disgusting."

That night, Tom and Diana made love for the last time.

He remembered holding her afterward, the blinds still open, moonlight showering their naked bodies. The world had felt perfect then.

He thinks about this night now and it is so far away.

He reaches out and only touches air. It is just him now.

Him and Victor.

"Please don't hurt her," Tom had pleaded, his chest bloody and pulsating from the gunshot. "Please, God."

Victor couldn't stop grinning, like they were playing some fucked-up game and he was winning. He pushed the gun deeper into Diana's skull. "I gotta admit, of all the fine lookin' bitches in this world, I think I may have struck gold."

"Please."

"Just think, man. Fuckin' anybody could have opened up, invited me inside. It could've been *anybody*. And that anybody just so happened to be your wife."

"No. No. No."

"You must have the world's shittiest luck." Victor laughed. "And me? I must have the best luck. *The best*."

"What do you want?" Tom said. "Dear God, what do you want?"

"I already got what I wanted, man. But shit. I guess a man's not a man once he stops prospecting, don't you say?"

Tom was silent. His body shook like an avalanche of sweat and tears and urine.

Victor grabbed Diana's hair and dragged her over to the radiator, leaving her next to David. David continued to cry through his duct tape. Victor took turns waving the gun in front of Diana and David.

The power of a firearm.

The magic of insanity.

The delusion of safety.

"I tell you what," Victor said, staring at Tom with wide, gleeful eyes. "Since we're having so much fun, I'll be nice. To let you in on a little secret, I was planning on killing both your girl and your kid here after I was finished with my business. I hadn't expected on anyone showing up and interrupting us. But that's okay. You didn't know."

"Please."

"But, *but* given that you've been *such* a good sport about all this, I figured, hey, why not throw you a bone?"

Tom was past the point of wanting to kill this intruder. He wanted to spill the blood of God and the rest of the universe. Fuck this whole existence.

"So here's what I'm gonna do," Victor said, still waving the gun back and forth. "I'm gonna tell you right off the bat. I can't leave here without at least killing *somebody*. That'd be cheating, and I'm a fair player. But I don't have to kill you all." He giggled. "You see what I'm saying? Not everybody here has to die today."

"What do you want me to do?" Tom's chest was on fire and he wondered how long it'd take until his heart surrendered. "Please, what . . . what do you *want?*"

Victor took a while to answer. He just started at Tom, smiling, in on a joke without a punch line.

Then he said, "I want you to choose."

And even though Tom immediately knew what he meant, he still said, "Wh-what?"

Victor pistol-whipped Diana and she fell on her stomach. Then he pointed the gun at David, Tom's boy, his own flesh and blood.

"I said, I want you to choose. It's pretty simple, you know? Who do you want to live? Who do you love more? Your wife, or your son?"

"Fuck you." Tom tried to stand, but his body was numb, useless. The volcano of blood pumping out of his chest had paralyzed him.

Victor laughed. "Look, dude, I don't have to be nice. I can just kill them both and leave. But I'm trying to do you a favor here, letting you pick one to keep. So come on. Don't make me regret this."

"No. Please. *No*."

Victor shrugged. "All right, whatever. No skin off my back. The both of them it is." He aimed the gun at Diana.

Tom screamed. Blood poured out of his mouth.

Victor paused, looked at him. "Have we come to a decision?"

After Victor was gone and Tom had managed to untie Diana, she started slapping him across the face and screaming, crying, calling him the worst names imaginable.

"Why didn't you pick me? *Why didn't you pick me?*"

All he could say was, "I love you, I'm sorry, I'm so sorry, I love you, I love you . . . "

Tom doesn't know if it's Victor's way of fucking him over even in prison that he's listed Tom's name under the allowed visitors, and he doesn't care. He hadn't even considered the possibility of not being allowed to see him. He'd driven the three hours to the prison in a daze. He'd driven out here before countless times, but he'd never had enough balls to actually get out of his car and walk inside.

Not until today.

Five years.

Fuck.

He sits behind the glass and waits a century. Eventually Victor walks out of his hiding spot and joins him on the other side of the glass. He's lost a lot of weight since the last time Tom'd seen him. He also now has a new scar across his face, as if one of his cellmates had tried extending his smile to his ears with a dull blade.

They sit in silence for many minutes, a wall of glass separating them. Tom can't bring himself to talk. After all this time, all the hours of practicing what he'd say, and he can't bring himself to even open his mouth.

Victor picks up the phone on his end and begins speaking. Tom doesn't know what he's saying, and he doesn't care. Today isn't about excuses or apologies. Today is about punishment.

Tom reaches into his pocket and pulls out two photographs, then presses them against the glass. As Victor leans forward for a closer look, Tom picks up his own phone and nestles it against his head.

He waits a good long while, allowing Victor time to stare at the photographs, one of Diana, the other of her new son. The son Victor had given her. Tears form in his eyes and drip down his cheeks. He looks away from the photographs and stares Tom in the eyes.

"No, man. No. You can't do this. Please. Oh, fuck. Please."

Tom says one word. The only word that matters anymore:

"Choose."

# THEY SAY THE SKY IS FULL OF SNAKEWOLVES

LUCY LEITNER

THE BRUISES HAVEN'T healed from the invisible finger grease on the wall incident, and he's already chasing her again. Ava runs up the stairs. Yeah, yeah, yeah. But when you live in a narrow row house, what are you going to do? There's nowhere to hide in the open kitchen/living room where the chase began. The unfinished basement offers no escape tunnels and has a lot less to pass the time than the bedroom. It's not like going outside is an option. At least the monster inside can be reasoned with. Maybe. And at least he's only one monster.

Ava crashes through the bedroom door and slams it shut, turns the lock. The dresser sits on soft pads to protect the precious hardwood floors. No other wood may touch them. No shoes either. Or knives. But it was Ava's running shoes that caused Jason to throw the knife, which missed her and lodged itself in the floor that precipitated this latest chase. The pads let the dresser slide with no resistance against the door. Jason crashes into the door. It doesn't budge. The lock does its job. Is it worth going "Here's Johnny" on his precious door? Ava hopes not, as the dresser will slide on its pads until it reaches the bed, leaving plenty of space for her fiancé to hurl himself into the room and resume the beatings that would continue until Ava's respect for his house improved. What would it be this time? A broken wrist? A shattered orbital socket like he'd threatened when he wielded the cast-iron skillet last week?

"Let me in, Ava." Jason must wish he didn't have that reverence for his home now. It would be liberating to crash through the door and tackle Ava onto the bed, grab her by the neck and bounce her skull on the wooden headboard until the lesson sunk in. But he won't do that, Ava hopes. Will he? "Every second I'm out here is only making it worse. You have so little respect for the floors, and now you're gonna make me destroy this door."

She's shaking. The swollen areas of her chest throb. Is that psychosomatic? The impact of the meat tenderizer he swung after she let bacon fat go down the drain had stopped hurting days ago. Is it the anticipation of new pain that makes the healing wounds hurt anew?

"Ava."

"No." She has so many words to say to him, but that's all she can let out beneath the thunderous heartbeat. It's as if her bruised chest is sucking itself in. Is it fear or anger? Does it matter?

As soon as she'd poured the fat into the sink, he was on her, swinging the metal hammer with its sharp little pyramids into her clavicle. Was it any less painful than taking the broom handle to the solar plexus after she'd hidden in the bathroom to let him "mellow out"? It was like a reverse Heimlich, one that made her feel that she was choking to death. The blisters from the scalding-water attack when the shower hair trap dislodged from the drain are now little white scars dotting her left arm. The ringing in her ear from that blow to the side of the head isn't dissipating.

It could be worse. He could hold her hand over the flame on the gas burner when ground beef sizzled out of the pan onto the pristine stainless steel range. The skin would burn red first, then turn to black as it charred more than the steak that had left an odor in the air that he feared would seep into the walls, prompting him to drag a steak knife over her forearm. If the house would be scarred, then so would Ava. The skin on her hand would melt away from the bone onto the greasy range, adding blood and plasma and liquefied collagen to the ground beef, thus necessitating another punishment. Maybe rape with the mop handle wasn't just a threat. Is today the day it will go that far? All she did was step onto the kitchen floor in her sneakers. Usually she slid the laundry basket onto the tiles and removed her shoes while still on the dusty, wooden steps. It wasn't the restored hardwood. Tile was easily cleaned. He mopped it twice a day. It wasn't the damage; it was the carelessness. She could never, ever slip. In this small house, his domain, she would never get away with anything. And with no escape, he could get away with everything.

Apologies and promises weren't working. She doesn't want to feel the mop handle.

She looks around the bedroom that doubles as her home office. Books, electronics, lamps. Everything would have to be thrown to fend him off. And Ava isn't Randy Johnson. The painting on the wall—shatter the glass and use the shard as a shiv? What good would that do when he has the rest of the house? The knives in the kitchen that he's already shown he'll use. The hammer in the basement where she would have run had the door locked (after the meat tenderizer incident, she'd researched her options). Even the fire extinguisher. Shit. She should have run into the bathroom. Shampoo shot into the eyes would be more effective than anything in here. No More Tears—hopefully that's false advertising.

"You're going to have to come out eventually. And I suggest you do it now. Before all the anger builds in me and I really think about the damage to the floor from that knife you made me throw."

There's nothing sharp in this room. It's just a bedroom/office where she sits all day on her connection to the world. The laptop! The tool that led her to him. She touches her fingertip to the keyboard, and the screen turns on. Yes! Her breathing slows.

He goes on. "I polish those floors every two weeks. Sweep every night. I'm on my hands and knees, picking up every little pebble you somehow manage to drag in every time you get a delivery. When you can't hang up your helmet and it drops on the floor, who's there buffing out the damage? You understand this was a last straw today. Your complete lack of respect for my property."

I knew it, Ava thinks. It's mop handle day. Well, it's the last straw for you too. Keep talking, she thinks. Keep talking, and you won't hear the keys clicking. She pulls up a browser. No connection. She stops breathing. Her line to the outside world severed. He must have unplugged the router, allowing her that second lead on him up the stairs but now trapping her here. There's no way out.

She should have listened to her mother. You can't know someone online. They can choose what to present to you. But Mom, I don't have your options. I can't just leave anytime I want like you could. You didn't have monsters outside when you met Dad.

It's not like the monsters sleep regular—or any consistent range of—hours. Even if I were to schedule a date, when would that be? We're all on call based on when the monsters decide to come out. And I'm not going on a date in my suit. Every inch of me covered in that loose silver foil. Even when it stops whooshing, you can't hear anything under the damn helmet.

Oh, don't get me started on the helmets, her mother had said.

Mom, we've been over this. You want the monsters to smell you? Come out of hiding and tear you apart? 'Cause that's what they do.

I know. Your Aunt Clare's podiatrist's godson—a lady from his church got ripped to shreds. Guts splattered all over the sidewalk, exploded like a bunch of kids were gonna start grabbing for candy. I heard the monsters tore through the suit. She was in ribbons. Her muscles hanging off the bones, face torn completely off. They found an eyeball a block away, still attached to all the nerves. They say it rolled all the way. Can you imagine? When they streamed the funeral, that must have been what they were all thinking. Tendons dangling out like she was wearing some sort of flapper dress, a shiny one with all that silver from the suit mixed into the entrails.

I know, Ma. That's why you gotta wear your helmet. The suits are just meant to conceal the smell of humans, not protect from the claws or fangs or talons or whatever it is the monsters use for their slicing and dicing.

Ava's helmet and suit are where they should be; in the closet by the front door. No way will she have time to slide into the jumpsuit, zip it all the way up to her chin, and strap on her helmet before Jason slashes her to bits. Which monster would she prefer? This one may fall asleep eventually. At least drift off on the couch long enough to knock him over the head.

How would she knock the monsters unconscious though? Do they even have heads? Are they eel-like creatures that slither up from the sewers or flying rats that hover above the clouds only to descend when they smell a human? Or does our scent create them anew each time? Are they the scaly snakewolves that her colleague Kendra's brother's optometrist's grandson saw out his window? How do you defend yourself from monsters you've never seen when you're cowering in a bedroom from a monster you promised to marry?

"We live in a palace!" he shouts, his voice cracking. He believes it. Has he not seen the interiors of other homes on video calls? The home tours that go viral on every social network? Yes, these videos can use tricks to make the homes seem more palatial than if you were to explore them in person, but that's an illusion we must face in our current situation. Were people able to disguise their homes as Jason disguised himself on the Monster Match dating app?

Everyone has a reality at home, inside, an existence disconnected from everyone else's. And this is mine, Ava thinks. Trapped in a well-kept row house with a man who transforms into a monster when she forgets to take off her shoes after a trip to the basement.

Jason would never cry over spilled milk, but he'd make sure Ava did.

She sits on the bed, grasping the lamp on the nightstand. She tosses off the shade. The base is lightweight, but stands about two feet tall. It would give her enough space to swing it at him without immediately being brought to the floor like the time her red hair dye—that color he said was so sexy in her Monster Match profile pic—dripped onto the white bathroom tile.

"Ava, it's becoming impossible to live with you like this." He sounds calmer, pleading even. "You don't appreciate how good you have it." Maybe that's true, she thinks. She's never known anything else.

The monsters unleashed their reign of terror when Ava was nine, before dating years in most states. It was no individual's fault, some sort of accident. Climate change. Cell towers. Factory farming. The Rothschilds. Opioids being flushed down the toilet and interacting with the fluoride that was already contaminating the water supply. Racists. Misinformation. Disinformation. Cisinformation. Everything that was for the worst in all possible worlds colliding and releasing unholy horror on them all.

It started where it always starts, in Florida. The headlines told a terrible story: "Florida Man Clawed to Bits in Walmart Parking Lot." The respectable papers didn't include the details, but they were easy to find on the internet. An ear was shredded like cheese; the crime lab analysts reconstructed it to the best of their abilities, but it appeared parts were taken by the assailant. The cheek was pierced to the bone, leaving the most extreme dimple one could imagine. The tongue was split in two, and the Adam's apple rolled through the parking lot until it was eventually squished by a motorized scooter. Bile spilled from the flayed stomach. It was too early in the morning for any witnesses—or more victims, as it turned out—as most of the Walmart customers did not take advantage of the store's 24-hour shopping.

At first, the law blamed the most likely culprit, another Florida Man. A fight over the importance of returning shopping carts to their tents had taken a bizarre and macabre turn. The second Florida Man was in custody when another outdoor shredding followed. The media blamed it on bath salts. Social media. Cults. Then similar reports came out of states they took seriously. The Oregon maulings started the mass panic. People stopped leaving their homes. They barely left for six months. When someone did, it would be on the news with a blanket over the corpse to protect viewers. No one was old enough to see how long an intestine really was.

Whatever cataclysmic event or set of circumstances unleashed the monsters is still up for debate. And it doesn't matter to most people. They stay inside. Leaving only in emergencies and always wearing their suits. They await the random sirens that alert them when the monsters sleep, allowing them to leave their homes. They step outside and rarely venture far from the door in case the second siren sounds to warn them the monsters have awakened.

They stay inside and live their lives through their on-screen avatars. Their little worlds are smaller, but everyone is just a tap away. That's how Ava ended up alone in this strange city with this monster. Monsters like Jason thrived. They could be anyone on the screens. It isn't until a lonely, naive woman moves across the county to live with them that they reveal the side that wields frying pans when you use the wrong mop.

Silence. Only the ringing in Ava's ear that has been there since the frying pan incident last month. She peers out the window. Gray, as usual. But no sign of any monsters. Just the desolate city street. Red brick houses filled with occupants she has never seen. They won't help her, the strange, likely hysterical woman who wants to invade their little sanctuary after destroying that of their neighbor. I'm Ava. Please let me in. I sometimes forget to take off my shoes, and my hair often falls out and collects in the carpet.

That won't do. No neighbors would allow someone like that to desecrate their world, the only part of the universe they can control.

She tiptoes from the bed to the door, turns her good ear toward it. Still silence. No breathing even from the other side. Maybe he has just gone to the bathroom on the other side of the landing. She waits. Minutes. No flush of a toilet. No running of the faucet. She keeps waiting, putting off the inevitable. Leaving this room may be the last time she has any agency. She leaves this room, she's at his whims, under his control. She stays here? Well, that puts her under his control as well. Remote control. Hah. And what is the plan when she does leave? She'll have to knock him unconscious, tie him up, and call the police. And hope he stays unconscious until they arrive. And that when they arrive, they believe her and her bruises and cauliflower ear.

Yes, that's the plan. It's better than any other. But she needs something to knock him unconscious, and the lamp isn't going to be it. Maybe. She bounces it up and down, gauging the weight. If she gets the right amount of torque, she can generate enough force to do some cranial damage. But he'll duck or block it before that can happen. Unless he can't see...

And she knows how to make that happen. She shakes again. The thought of the knife plunging into the wood floor inches from her foot. Yes, she's wearing her running shoes, but they won't stop the blade from piercing flesh and cutting bone. She could deal with the bruises and the hearing loss, but her feet are the only freedom she's known since she was nine years old.

She breathes in deep, closes her eyes, tries to remember more calming hacks she's seen online. Her heart rate slows enough to let her stand without her legs wobbling. She slides the dresser back away from the door. She unlocks it as slowly as possible, hoping to eliminate any sort of click. Grasping the lamp base, she pushes it open. No creak. At least the spatula spanking she'd endured had led to the positive effect of his fixing that.

The landing is empty. A noise is coming from downstairs. She doesn't know what it is, and it doesn't matter. All that matters is she knows where he is.

She tiptoes into the bathroom, locking the door behind her. Beneath the sink is an array of cleaning products, Jason's collection. Each serves its own special purpose and is to be used in a distinct order. If that system is violated, her head goes in the toilet. At least she knows the water will be clean. She'd listened so carefully to Jason's instructions she hadn't read the labels. All she looks for now in the fine print is a warning: Avoid eye contact. The spray bleach will work. Bleach and a lamp. She looks at her reflection in the mirror. She would laugh if it weren't so sad.

Behind the showerhead in the freestanding, claw-foot tub is a closet. At least, she assumes it's a closet. It could be a secret passage to a fantasy world for all she knows. He'd said to never look inside, that he was kind enough to share his home with her but he needed some space to himself. He'd said that before the terror began. She'd obeyed. She would have respected that, she tells herself, even without the threats he always made good on. But now, she can't leave a potential weapons cache un-searched.

She pulls the door open. It isn't a closet, but a pantry with five shelves. Now it's obvious why he wanted to keep it secret. It's a mess. The white paint cracks off the shelf edges. Some sort of substance that looks sticky, but she doesn't want to touch to confirm, was spilled on the second shelf from the top. It's such an unkempt disaster, so incongruous with the rest of the house, that she almost fails to notice the bones. Fingers. Clean finger bones. No flesh, no tissue. None of the carnage the monsters leave behind outside. So tidy these bones, like the rest of the house. Five of them, each threaded through a ring. Ava looks down at her left hand, though she doesn't need to. She already knows, but she needs to make sure her eyes aren't deceiving her. Yes, it's identical to the engagement ring he'd given her when she moved in. He's like a Russian doll of monsters.

She has just lost her choice. Either she beats him and ties him up or she holds her finger down on the bleach trigger and empties the bottle in his nose and mouth until it eats away his insides.

The bottle in one hand, the lamp in the other, she leaves the bathroom. She walks down the steps. It doesn't matter what noise she makes; the open staircase that he somehow hasn't thrown her from yet will reveal her soon enough. She sees him first, right off the bottom of the steps, just before the kitchen. He pushes the floor buffer over the cut where the knife had plunged. He looks up at her and raises the buffer over his shoulder like a baseball bat.

"I hope you're here to help remove the damage that you've done to the floor. This buffer is doing a pretty good job of getting a knife wound out of hardwood. Imagine what it could do to your face."

In a split second, Ava raises the bleach bottle and shoots it at his face. He shouts and blinks his eyes shut. Blind, he swings the buffer. She hops off the staircase to the open side in the living room and runs for the door. His right eye is shut, and those involuntary tears run down his cheek, but the left is wide open. He walks toward her, the buffer raised. She drops to the floor in a squat. Why? She doesn't know. He swings it down, catches her shoulder. She shouts in pain, and the bottle falls out of her grasp. He raises the buffer again with both hands behind his head, like he's about to swing a sledgehammer. She hops up and shoves him back while his arms are in the air. The weight of the buffer sends him back. He drops it behind him so he doesn't fall. He lunges at her, but she meets him with the bulb end of the lamp. The thin glass shatters in his T-shirt. She pulls it back and stabs it at his heart. The tiny glass shards aren't enough to penetrate deeper than the dermis, but it's enough to send him back. And enough time to run the five feet to the front door.

Fuck it. She'll take her chances with the monsters. It's better than giving this one the satisfaction. The monsters out there can't help it.

She unlocks the door and runs through. She runs down the middle of the desolate street, past the other row houses. She covers a block before she turns back. No one is on the street. No maniac swinging a floor buffer over his head. She keeps running straight down the street in the gray twilight. Thirteenth Street, 14th, 15th, 16th. She's never run this far before. She usually takes her jogs in her suit and helmet in laps around the block in case the sirens sound that the monsters have awakened. She keeps running. Nineteenth, 20th. Still no one behind her. She slows to a walk, looks around the neighborhood she's never seen, all these neighbors who may as well be worlds away.

In her fear of the monster inside the house, she forgot about the monsters outside. The monsters with the faces of wolves and bodies of snakes that used their giant claws to rip all humans to shreds and send chunks of tissue flying into neighbors' stoops. Or the scale-covered anthropoids with their vampire fangs that turn human legs into hula skirts. The monsters that are unleashed by the smell of humans. The monsters that she has feared since her mother told her about her godmother's sister's manicurist's nephew's accountant who went out to retrieve a package that had blown off the porch and returned with his arm ripped out at the socket, blood spraying the living room, drenching his poor, screaming wife until he finally collapsed on the carpet. During the early days, before the authorities understood how the monsters sleep, bodies could sit for weeks. Ava heard all about the one-armed, decomposing corpse, how the flesh turned green after a couple of days, the stiff cadaver turning squishy and liquefying right there in the living room. The stench of blood and voided bowels and rot soaking into the carpet, along with the fluids that used to keep him alive. By the time the cleanup crew finally arrived, he had seeped through the rug and left an asymmetrical body print on the hardwood floor beneath.

It was those monsters that stopped Ava from having a life at nine years old, that led her to Jason. So, where are they?

She stands in the middle of the empty street, breathing in the cool air that tastes so different from the air in the house, poisoned by floor buffers and bleach and elbow grease and bones. Time flies by as she breathes in the air with no anxiety about a pending siren for the first time in 15 years. Standing still, lacking all vigilance, she's like monster bait. But none comes. No claws. No breeze of rancid breath that the few survivors claimed. Silence. Peace. A feeling she needs to share.

"Neighbors! The monsters are dead!" Ava shouts. She runs up and down the street. "There are no monsters! Come outside! Live your life!"

She stops in the center of the street and spins, her arms outstretched, welcoming in this big, new world.

Bang.

Ava falls, in one motion sideways onto the street. The thud and the crack sound at the same time. Blood seeps from the hole in her head. It makes the blacktop look wet.

The two men in silver suits approach. One carries a rifle over his shoulder. The other bends down and raises Ava's wrist in his silver-gloved hand. It's hard for the man with the gun to hear the other from beneath their helmets.

"She's dead."

"And I pray for her. But we can't let her wake the monsters. Remember, son, we must remain vigilant. You don't want to be the next one scalped in the street. Never forget about your grandfather's golfing buddy's pastor's son's transvestite lover and how the thing stuck its claws up his nostrils and pulled his face right off. Remember how a bird flew away with his bloody wig and used it to make a nest while the monsters ripped at his faceless body, pulling his brain out through the cleared-out nasal passage just like they did in ancient Egypt. Blood and snot and gray matter everywhere. Now is that what you want, Son?"

"No, Dad."

"Then shoot her again. Make sure she's dead."

# THE END OF TIME ON ROSEWYLD LANE

JAY WILBURN

I HOPE THEY find my seven-year-old son dead and decomposed down to the dirty bones soon. I hope he's so far gone by now that they have to identify him from dental records and there's nothing left to clue into what he suffered before his body was hidden. I pray for this at least once a day whether God still listens or not. I've never meant a prayer more in my life. If he won't answer that one, I might switch it up and ask that I'm found dead soon. I don't care so much where or how, but as far as the when goes, Jesus Fucking Christ, let it be soon.

I pass the turn for our street sort of by accident and sort of on purpose. I make the next left off Samsonn Courte onto Hollend Avenue. This street has grassy medians full of flowers. Shit, is it time for flowers to bloom again? My wife is going to be beside herself. More than usual, I mean.

Goddamn it, I don't want to believe this is what usual is for us now, but I guess that's exactly what it is.

I miss him. We all do, of course. It goes without saying. My wife is a shell of her former self.

Cameryn misses the hell out of her younger brother too. She comes alive a little around her friends, but there is still a darkness in her, a storm that never stops brewing behind her eyes. I'd love it if she'd lash out at me like my wife has a few times. I don't want another female in the house screaming at me, but it would be good to see that storm break inside her before it eats her alive, before it turns her into her mother, I guess I mean. When she's at home, all that life drains out of her in an instant. It makes me fear that any glimmer of happiness she shows away from our family is more of an act and the brooding, lost girl that stares through things instead of at them is the reality. There are boys who prey on brokenness like that.

God help us, the world is full of fucking predators hunting every street in the world.

I reach the northern end of Hollend. Without much thought, I turn west on Absynthe Way. I want to say that street is named after a drink laced with opium, but I don't know. I feel like I'm in a drugged haze as I wave at the Philmoors working in their yard, all their kids accounted for. They're good parents. Better than me, I suppose. My absent son used to play with their kids. Such a little boy to haunt such a wide stretch of streets and life.

Fuck.

I should have been paying attention. I should have known better. Everyone tells me it's not my fault. My wife doesn't say it and my daughter doesn't say it anymore, but everyone else does. I can't believe it though because the truth hurts, and I need to punish myself with the kind of truth that hurts the most. Forgiving myself for something like this feels wormy and rotten, like a body hidden in the woods after God knows what.

We were loading up the car for a family trip that day. It wasn't the Disney trip. That was supposed to be in December—December two years ago. Cameryn was being nasty about having to go, but her brother was all joy. He stood on top of a root and called for his sister to look at him balance. She held up her hands beside her head and shook them, her eyes bulging with older sibling frustration.

As we loaded her bike on the rack behind the van. He was riding his bike around and singing a song about the pirate's life being for him. I don't even know where he heard it. On YouTube or in memes, I guess. She kept yelling at him to shut up. I took her aside and talked to her about being kind to him. I said that in the future they would need to count on each other because we wouldn't always be around, most of her friends now wouldn't be in her life forever, but her brother would always be there for her. I actually said that shit on that day. I think that last scolding haunts her too. I know it's a permanent sour taste in the back of my throat.

On his next loop around our driveway, I told him we needed to load up his bike and he said, "One more time around."

I didn't say yes or no, but I let him go as we packed other things. Some people tell me it's a false memory, a manifestation of my guilt after the fact, but I don't think so. I distinctly remember thinking that something might happen to him while we were fucking around with the car. I mostly thought about him getting hit by a car, but that underpinning fear of your kid getting grabbed by someone was bubbling under the surface of my mind then too.

Our street is sort of a culdesac and sort of not. There are trails for golf carts and hiking, but a couple are wide enough for cars. It's a maze of those trails through the little wooded areas between streets. People should have seen if he was taken up one of them, but no one did.

It was my fucking responsibility to keep up with him, not theirs.

A car honks behind me and wakes me up from my fugue. There's no light where Absynthe meets the four lanes plus a middle turn of Coremyyn

Highway, but I'm sitting there like I'm waiting on one. I don't bother waving an apology, but pull across two lanes in a gap in traffic that is probably a little too tight and drive south, going slow in the fast lane.

He didn't come back and he didn't come back as we finished packing. I finally walked out to the end of the drive and called him like a dog. I walked out and tried to hunt him down, but he'd already been hunted. We found the bike, but not him. I ran around calling for him until the neighbors came out. They started calling and spreading out in an unorganized search. Most of them would join the official organized search that would follow, but would turn up nothing. It felt like forever, but it was probably only five minutes before I called the police in a panic. One of the neighbors had to take the phone and relay the information for me, because I couldn't hold it together.

I expected the police to say they had to wait before they started looking, but they looked right away for what it was worth. They found one neighbor growing pot in their basement. They found another senile old lady neglecting animals. They found a guy hiding in his girlfriend's house with an out of state warrant for car theft. But they never found my son.

He expressed so much joy that day and it was the last he ever felt.

There's a light at the turn for Samsonn Courte. I ease into the turn lane, get the arrow pretty quickly, and travel east toward our street again.

I expected them to suspect me. They always suspect the father or husband in cases like this. If they ever did, they never said anything.

I walked those cart trails forever. I was always looking for a shoe. I don't know why exactly, but I always expected to find one of his shoes. I reminded myself to not touch it, just to call the police, but I never found anything all those combing search parties failed to find.

I drove around, sometimes alone, sometimes with my wife, with the van still packed like we were just going to find him, pick him up, and take that trip. I don't even remember when we finally unpacked. We never stopped looking though. We never packed up his room. We still have that bike in the garage if he comes back at age nine to sing of pirates' lives again.

We canceled Disney. He vanished before November 1st, so we were able to get all our money back on deposits.

I hold the steering wheel tighter and tighter until my knuckles turn white like the old cliché. I grit my teeth until my jaw hurts. I pass our street again and signal the turn north up Hollend Avenue yet again.

I floated the idea late last year for my wife and Cameryn going to Disney again maybe with some of Cameryn's friends. A girls' weekend or hell, two weeks, if they wanted. Cameryn's still young enough for it. She'd be away from home and with her friends, the conditions under which she is most alive, even if the darkness remains behind the eyes. That idea went nowhere. My wife didn't even bother to run it by our daughter for her opinion.

I know what she's thinking. If we went to Disney and he showed back up at the house finally to find his family had moved on without him . . .

He used to have dreams. Nightmares. He used to have nightmares.

Left on Absynthe. I pass the Philmoors again. No one waves this time. I can't remember how many times I've passed them, but it's more than once today, and I've followed this same flight path on previous occasions.

In one nightmare, he wakes up to find the house empty. We've gone to Disney without him and he's sad. I don't know if my wife remembers him telling us this, but I do.

In another nightmare, one that occurred closer to his disappearance, the doorbell rings. We had and still have one of those fancy smart doorbells with a camera that announces through the speakers, "Someone is at door."

He imitated the voice perfectly when he was telling us the story. It gave me chills. It gives me a chill every time I hear it now. My wife runs to the door every time like she expects it to be him. I want to get rid of it, but we don't change anything at our house anymore.

In his dream, he went to check the door and no one was out there. He goes to look for us and all three of us are gone.

The doorbell rings again with that voice echoing through the nightmare version of our house. This time, a man in a mask busts through the door with a knife trying to stab him.

I go south on Coremyyn Highway and ease into the turn lane to wait on the light.

Goddamn it all, I know he thought of those dreams when he was grabbed by whoever took him. I fucking know it. His greatest fear revealed in that nightmare world in his head was that we wouldn't be there and we weren't. I wasn't.

Left on Samsonn.

I used to see kids on milk cartons, kids on posters, kids on the back of junk mail shoppers, kids on missing person shows rolled out for our morbid entertainment, and I felt nothing. I don't feel much now, but I feel the terrifying void of his absence.

Passed my turn to the most haunted house on the fucking Earth.

There is something horrific in the nightmare world of "missing" that can't be matched with all the horror movie splatter that the sickest minds in the fantasy world of special effects can produce. I might feel differently if they finally find what remains of him, but I doubt it.

Left onto Hollend. The goddamn flowers are blooming.

He's not alive. He's not dead. He's a fucking unanswered question.

It's the most indescribably painful emptiness, that unanswered question.

Left on Absynthe. The Philmoors have gone inside to keep their children safe from the rolling cloud of curse that surrounds me, a curse that makes children vanish without a trace.

We can't move on. We're not allowed to. Because he could be. He can't be, of course, I know that, but I'm not allowed to admit that. People are found in basements in places like Cleveland all the time, so why not here?

South on Coremyyn. A truck swerves to miss me, laying down on his horn. I don't even flinch. I hope someone you love goes missing.

I will never think of him as nine because he'll never stop being seven. Never. When we talk about him to others, he's nine now. If I slip up and say he was seven, my wife won't forgive that. Our marriage is probably doomed anyway, but that slip-up would speed it along. Who are we to thrive and survive when our innocent little boy wasn't allowed to?

Left onto Samsonn and I already know I'm passing our street again before I get there. No white-knuckled anticipation this time.

If I allow myself to fully let go, even for the sake of healing, and he did turn up, the police did bring him back to us alive, how could I forgive that? I gave up on him just like in his darkest nightmares where someone was at the door and we weren't there to save him.

Left on Hollend without even having to think about it. I hope no kid comes running out into the street because I'm barely paying attention. Take your children inside and keep them safe, you fools.

If I hold onto him and pretend it is hope, but he never returns again, I'll be tortured my entire life, but that's what I deserve because I fucked up. It's my fault. I failed him.

Left on Absynthe. The street is deserted. No witnesses if someone else is snatched. The fucking Philmoors in their house safe with their safe kids, I'd trade every last one of them to get my son back or to even get proof he's dead at this point.

I don't even want to believe he is still alive because I can't allow myself to imagine the living nightmare he'd have to be in. Sure, some bereaved mother who lost her baby might have grabbed him as a replacement. He might be brainwashed to believe we are gone and she's his real mother. He might grow old and one day find us with a family of his own, all that missing life partially paid for in the end. Maybe we'll all make that belated trip to Disney finally with our new grandkids.

But—left onto Coremyyn Highway—that's never going to happen.

Because that's not what happened. I know it in my heart.

If he's still alive, he's going through unspeakable torture. He's alone in his worst nightmare where we're just gone and he's on his own with the masked monster that keeps him like an animal, like a toy. Worse than death if he's been in a joyless hell for the last two years.

Left on goddamned Samsonn.

I'd rather imagine his bones in soil that's fed by his rotten flesh.

Missed the turn again. Surprise. There's a haunted house down there waiting on a haunted street. There's a bicycle but no boy to go with it. If there is a boy, he's too big for that bike by now, but nothing changes on that street, in that house. Not a fucking thing. All the clocks went tick but never tock.

No one is allowed to feel joy again. The missing boy was the last one to feel it, in fact.

Hollend, Absyhthe, Coremyyn, Samsonn, Hollend, Absynthe . . .

I realize to my horror that I really am paying attention. My head hurts from my eyes darting back and forth so much. I'm looking around. I'm looking for him. Sometimes I'm looking for a shoe still, but I'm looking for him. I'm looking for him at seven years old so I can put him in the car, buckle him in, and take him home. I'm still driving around looking. Because he's never aged. Because time is holding its breath for his precious soul.

I need to make that turn I keep skipping. The house isn't haunted, I am. I carry that with me, and I can't get away from myself as they say in recovery.

I need to tell my wife I love her. I need to tell my daughter it's okay to keep living. I need to take us back to family therapy even if we hate it more than Cameryn hated the idea of that final trip we never took.

If I had just said no to one more time around, loaded his bike, and took off down the road away from whatever predator hunted our street that day, just until he moved on or took someone else's kid, one I didn't give a shit about . . . fucking if . . .

Someone was at the door.

I need to take responsibility for the family I still have waiting on the clocks to finally go tock. But I won't. I will finally make that turn and pull into the driveway. I'll go inside and go through the motions. But there will be no "I love you" and no "let's start to heal." That would be a change and we don't change anything in that house because he might come back one day. And unlike in all his nightmares, we'll be there when he does. We'll be there with Mom's empty eyes and his sister's stormy ones.

And me. I'll be there. The guy who failed to keep him safe will be there.

Shit. I miss my turn on Hollend Avenue where the flowers bloom again. I'll have to circle back.

Until the hanging question of our son is answered, we'll be there waiting.

# NEW FOX SMELL

## LIVIA LLEWELLYN

"You're going to be fine. It's just a month."

Laurel's mother speaks to her from behind the screen door. Laurel turns and gives her a tight-lipped smile. The screen metal is thick and gray, and her mother looks like she's floating within a rectangular storm.

"All of August," Laurel says. "I'll come back and have to start school right away, I won't have any time to get ready."

"I don't understand you, we've already been over this. You wanted to be invited, I remember how you begged Patricia."

"That was *years* ago, mom. You know we haven't been friends since seventh grade."

"All the cool girls get invited to the island, you used to say. I'll just die if I don't go, you said. I thought you'd be happy that she invited you, that we agreed to let you go."

"You mean make me go, and for four whole fucking weeks. And once again, I had to quit my job!"

Laurel waits for her mother to shout *language!* like she always does, but instead she pushes the wooden front door closer to the screen, her face growing darker as it recedes into the house. "You told us you wanted to go on vacation, so now you're going. It's done," she says, every word dripping with the implication that Laurel is already gone, her absence both welcome and irreversible. She's already looking away, to the living room, the kitchen. Laurel knows she should be used to this, but the pain and anger always surprise her as they flare up once again, flooding her body with cold prickly blood; and for a brief second, she's overcome with the thrill and relief of leaving this house, running as far as she can from this sticky, predictable cage of a life.

A car horn blares, the second time since Mrs. Gibson steered her massive Cadillac into their small driveway. A pale hand adorned with diamonds and gold beckons from behind the fogged windshield. Rain falls down all around them, smacking through waxy rhododendron leaves and pattering against the sides of the house.

"We'll take good care of her, Marcy," Mrs. Gibson shouts as her makeup-perfect face emerges from the driver-side window. Little gold hoops glint from her ears. "Patty's going to be so happy to have her there. It's all she's talked about this summer—honestly, if I hadn't agreed to come back to the mainland to fetch you, I don't know what she'd have done."

Her mother's voice, behind her. "Remember to say thank you. And stop worrying, Patricia's still your best friend. Maybe you'll have so much fun you won't ever want to come back home again." The front door closes quietly, but the bolt locks sound like gun shots.

"Don't you wish," Laurel mutters, and picks up the suitcase resting at her feet. It's her old baby suitcase, covered in bright pop-art daisies and peeling travel stickers from all the interesting places they vacationed at every summer. That was long ago, though, and Mom and Dad didn't see the need to get new suitcases for something they don't want to do anymore. Well, do with her. Laurel was more fun when she was five, her father once admitted. She's seventeen now, and hasn't been fun for years, apparently.

"Hurry up, honey, it's a long drive and we want to get there before dark!" Mrs. Gibson, shouting out the window of the car. Laurel grabs the handle and runs to the car. The passenger door swings open and she tips the suitcase into the back seat before sliding in.

"Seatbelt on. Don't want you flying through the window." Mrs. Gibson smiles as they back out of the driveway and up the street. Laurel straps herself in, then wipes at her wet face, pinching her nose slightly before wiping her hands on her jeans. The car smells like damp pleather and upholstery and chemical-soaked car fresheners, all the normal car smells. But beneath those scents, her nose picks up a sulfurous layer of rotting vegetables and moldering earth, and the sharp musk of unwashed crotch and wet animal fur.

"Those are a lot of trees." Laurel flicks at the three fresheners swinging from the front view mirror, then swivels in her seat. She counts at least seven—no, nine—more hanging throughout the car.

"It just gets harder every year to get all the smells out."

"I'm sure." Laurel presses her lips together, trying not to breath too deep. A fire wouldn't get rid of those horrible scents. "But wait, isn't this a new car? I mean, this isn't your other car. I feel like I see Patricia in a different car every time I see her. I can't keep track."

"It's really doing a number out there," Mrs. Gibson mutters. They turn onto the avenue, heading toward the bridge. "But the weather is always better on the island."

"I've noticed that Patricia always comes back to school with a tan,"

Laurel says. *Along with a new car, and always new friends. Nothing ever old for her.*

"She does indeed."

They both fall silent. Houses and businesses rush by on both sides of the avenue, neon signs and traffic lights twinkling in the downpour. Laurel rests her elbow against the edge of the car door, her hand a fist against her face as if she's knocking herself out. She thinks about the small, laidback hippie grocery story she'd been working at since June, the job she had to quit for this. Last year she had to leave a highly-coveted job as a barista so her parents could send her to a two-week horse camp somewhere in the lower folds of Mount Rainier; the summer before that it was volunteer work with a group of obscenely cheerful church kids in Eastern Washington, for which she gave up shelving books at the local library. She just wanted *one* ordinary, stupid summer like all her friends had, like scooping ice cream into papery cones at Farrell's or hanging limp dresses onto hangers in some gross mall store, hanging out after work in hot parking lots, smoking and bitching about the next school year. But Laurel's not stupid. Whenever she leaves for one of these arranged adventures, her parents get the house to themselves. They get to pretend she'd never been born. Sometimes she wonders if she should be pretending the same thing.

"Patty will be so happy to see you. She gets a little lonely on the island during the summer. But the house has been in my husband's family for generations, and it's expected."

"What's expected?" Laurel asks.

"Oh, it's just tradition, to always spend summer on the island. It's actually very pleasant, the house is quite nice. You can have your own room, or you can share one of the larger rooms with Patricia, or you can both stay in one of the cottages. There's a nice little library and a big kitchen, a tennis court and pool near the gardens, and plenty of beaches for walking. They're gravel beaches, though. Driftwood and stones. The entire island, nothing but a ring of driftwood and stones and evergreens. Long trails and animal runs through the evergreens . . . " Mrs. Gibson's voice fades, and the squelching of the windshield wipers fills the space. They're now making their way onto the Narrows Bridge, the thump-thump-thump of each steel-plated section beating like a giant heart under the tires. Every now and then the car gives a sudden small swerve to the left or right as Mrs. Gibson steers it over the metal grates, and all Laurel can think about is the car continuing that swerve, sliding across the lanes and flipping over the railings, sailing through the gray air into the icy churning waters of the Straits below. She grabs the straps of her seat belt, clenching the hard fabric until her fingers hurt.

"I'm surprised Patricia gets lonely, I thought she always invites a bunch of friends over. I'm not the only one in her class who's going to be there, right?" Laurel doesn't really care, but anything to get her mind off the fact that they're speeding on a narrow metal strip suspended in the middle of the air, and that Mrs. Gibson's pupils are as wide as a cat's.

"Oh, well, yes, she always invites a few girlfriends over every June, and my sister and two brothers all have teenagers around yours and Patty's age, so there's always some of their friends in the house, but most of them are gone before August. To be honest, most of them are gone by the end of June—none of them are ever quite up for surviving island life. Aside from her cousins, Patty's always the last one in her circle still standing, so to speak. My little baby fox, all by herself, as usual." Mrs. Gibson chuckles slightly, and pats Laurel's knee, a friendly "just between us girls" gesture Laurel has experienced from older women more times in her life than she cares to count. She responds with her usual knowing smile.

"What's to survive, it sounds wonderful. An island all to yourselves, a tennis court, a pool. I'm surprised Patricia would ever want to leave."

"Well, yes, but there's no town, of course. So we have to import all our necessities and our pleasures. And you young folks always get bored after a few days and want to go shopping or see movies or whatever it is you do. So I suppose what seems peaceful and cozy to us feels like hell to others, if you're not used to it."

"I think I could get used to it. I mean, it doesn't sound like I'll get bored. At any rate, I don't plan on leaving until the end of the summer."

"I do hope so. You would be the first."

The fuzzy curve of the bridge flattens out, and the cables dwindle down to nothing on either side: they're on solid land again, back on the planet, and Laurel's fingers loosen their grip on the seatbelt. She quietly lets out a long breath which she hadn't realized she'd been holding in. Once again, she relaxes, watches trees and strip malls whoosh past in a continuous blur. They're at the outer edges of the Olympic Peninsula, the soft, civilized areas where the wealthy have settled, pouring money into electrical grids and sewer systems and any kind of expensive architecture that makes them forget that they do not really belong in this part of the world. Laurel feels herself slipping into light sleep, the sleep of traveling, where her body floats in and out of some other part of the universe, impervious to movement and the passage of time, while in the present the car and road and world whirl around her paralyzed flesh in a muted roar.

"No real foxes," Mrs. Gibson murmurs. "Not for years."

Laurel's head snaps up. "I'm sorry, what," she mumbles as she grabs at the seatbelt, which has cinched itself tighter during her short (or was it long?) nap. She stretches her legs out as far as they can go, her sneakers tapping at the curved shell of the interior. Laurel was never a patient traveler—the longer they drive, the more the car seems to cinch itself around them. The rain has slowed to a more typical drizzle, speckling the windows just enough that Mrs. Gibson has to hit the wiper button every couple of minutes to clear the glass. There's no other cars on the highway, it's just them, a speck of metal sailing down the empty ribbon of concrete underneath an ocean of clouds. Up ahead, the highway disappears along with the trees into the horizon. It's like they're sailing into space.

"I'm so sorry, dear, I thought you were awake. I was saying, there aren't any actual foxes on the island."

"Oh?"

"Just so there's no expectations on your part. Everyone's always disappointed there's no foxes. They disappeared a long time ago. Of course, every summer we bring a few new strains over, but they never seem to survive the transplant more than a few days, a week at the most. It's not an easy place for them to live, I guess, when will this damn rain end?" Mrs. Gibson squints and juts her face at the windshield, coated with a river of droplets despite the squealing efforts of the wipers. Outside, most of the traffic has bled away into the surrounding towns and villages hidden beyond the wide edges of the highway. A strange thought blossoms inside Laurel, her curiosity tinged with a sudden fear.

"Wait, why don't they survive? What's on the island that kills the foxes?"

Mrs. Gibson cocks her head and smiles, then gives a quick shrug of her shoulders, as if she couldn't say. "I guess . . . I guess they spend so much time being angry that they were tricked onto a strange island that they don't teach themselves how to adapt and survive. They just run around, screaming like children until they're too weak to run or fight."

"Fight what, bears? Please don't tell me there are bears."

"No, dear. Not bears. You'd never guess in a million years."

"Huh." A small huff of air shoots through Laurel's nostrils as it dawns on her. "You hold fox hunts. Your family hunts foxes every summer. Is that it? Is that why all Patricia's friends leave so soon? Because they won't kill the foxes?"

"Patty said you've always thought of yourself as very clever. Very leader of the pack clever. A good quality to have, although now that I think about it, I'm not sure she meant it as a compliment."

Laurel swivels her body around as much as she can in the miniscule space. "Wow. You know, Mrs. Gibson, Patricia and I haven't really been close friends for a couple of years now. I mean, I can't imagine what she'd have to say about me, she doesn't really know who I am anymore. I don't even know why she invited me. But I can tell you right now that I'm not going on any fox hunt. I mean, if she remembers anything about who I am, she'd know that."

Mrs. Gibson places a ringed hand on Laurel's sweaty knee and gives it a firm squeeze. "You have my word, Laurel, you won't have to touch a single gun."

"Thank you."

Laurel stares out the window again. They've long passed the remnants of human life, and the freeway is an unbroken line, no cut-offs or exits anywhere in sight. The trees rush past in a wall so unbroken, so symmetrical, that for a dizzying second it feels as if they're driving down the same stretch of road past the same hundred yards of forest over and over again, caught in an endless loop. She remembers when she and Patricia and the other kids used to play in the woods just outside their neighborhoods, the few remaining stretches of undeveloped land in a region where the cities grew faster and further and more destructive than clouds of volcanic ash. They ran through those woods like animals, tearing through massive ferns and soaring over fallen branches, weaving their way toward the rough rocky beaches of the Straits where they fell about, panting and staring up at the storm grey skies. As much as they've grown apart, Laurel still misses those days, filled with the crash of their feet against the forest floor, their hot panting in the cool, clean air, the echoing silence of the wide world pouring over and through and past them, making them small and enormous all at once. Laurel leans her head against the window again, ignoring the cramping in her legs and hips from the uncomfortably small seat. That damp, sour-sharp smell has only grown stronger, even the grove of swinging tree fresheners can't hold it at bay. She's drowning in the scents, in the cloying, overheated air.

"I'm just curious. If you aren't friends any longer, why did you accept the invitation?"

"I didn't want to go," she finally mumbles. Her head lolls down. "My parents wanted me out of the house, they made me go. I don't want to go."

*Oh, I don't believe that.* Mrs. Gibson's voice sounds millions of miles, millions of years away. *I don't believe that at all. You're just like my Patty. I've seen you run.*

Her fingers are buzzing. That's what draws her away from the river of fever-dream half-sleep, where her limp body was floating above a grey, tree-lined road stretching toward a bluish bump hovering far up above the edge of the earth, nestled in a secret layer of space between the stars. Laurel blinks her gummy eyes, drawing her cramped hand out of her pocket. A notification bar on her phone is flashing, but she can't read the words, they don't look like any language she's ever seen before. Outside it's still late afternoon, time has passed yet still they're making their way down what feels like that same stretch of six-lane highway that cuts through that same solid wall of evergreens, now crowded against the flat edges of the concrete barriers as if slowly and steadily resisting the intrusion, pressing back until they can once again flow uninterrupted across their own lands.

"No phone service anymore. Not here. Go back to sleep." Mrs. Gibson's languid voice cuts through the fuzz: Laurel slides up in her seat, wincing as she lets her right arm, stiff and tingling from being curled up against her head for so long, drop slowly back down to her side.

"I wasn't really sleeping." She can barely push the words out of her phlegm-coated mouth. Is she sick? "I thought we'd be there already."

"Everything is further out, out here. You know how it is."

Laurel doesn't respond. She's struggling to shake off the drugged, cottony feeling in her head, and the smell in the car has grown. It's angry, powerful and musky, so cloyingly strong it makes her eyes water and her heart flail in her chest. The entire car feels smaller, as if the odors are compressing everything around her. Laurel reaches to her side, fumbling for the window button in the door. It doesn't yield to her touch.

"I think—I think this is stuck?" she asks, pressing down so hard it feels like she's going to snap the bone. "It's so stuffy, I don't feel good, I need fresh air."

"All the fresh air is on the island. Stay calm. Be still. Go back to sleep."

"Please, I feel like I can't breath—maybe one of the back windows?" Laurel glances over at Mrs. Gibson. A faint smile is frozen on the woman's lipstick-pink mouth. Other than the slight movement of her chest rising and falling with each breath, she seems almost motionless, as though a picture of Mrs. Gibson sits beside her. So close to her now, as if they were about to hug. Laurel looks down. Her car seat is so small that her thighs spill over its edges, and her knees are firmly jammed against the underside of the dashboard. She raises her hand, placing a palm flat against the ceiling of the car, now only an inch above her head, if even that.

"Did we switch cars?" The words aren't even out of her mouth before Laurel realizes how absurd they are.

Mrs. Gibson laughs as she sits back, her face and posture natural again, relaxed. "You didn't smoke something before I picked you up, did you? It's fine, I know how girls your age just love to experiment."

Laurel can't be bothered to smile anymore. Despite the numbing effects of all the scents, she feels cold panic rising inside her, and resists the urge to buck her legs out, smash her fists against the window, anything to make more room. "No, no, it's not that. It's—something's wrong. Something's wrong with the car." She places her hand on the glove compartment, sliding her thumb over the latch that's almost next to her stomach. "And I thought we'd be there by now."

"As soon as we get to ferry at the end of the bridge."

Laurel is silent. Something about that statement is terribly wrong. She shakes her head, but she can't shake off the fuzzy confusion seeping across her eyes, across her mind. Her mouth opens and closes, then opens again. "A ferry?"

"Of course! It's an island, how do you think we get to it?"

"Right, yeah. Still sleepy, I guess." Laurel rubs her eyes, then tugs at a hairband around her wrist. Her fingers can barely work their way under the band, all her energy has bled into the damp, cloying air. She lets her hands drop into her lap and stares at them. They look like two dead spiders. Her phone slides onto the floor with a dull thump. She doesn't have the strength to bother.

"It doesn't make sense," she mutters at her hands.

"What dear?" Mrs. Gibson asks.

"If the island is connected by a bridge, why are we taking a ferry?"

Mrs. Gibson lets out a long yawn. "There's no bridge to the island, only to the ferry. Only the ferry can get to the island."

"What? I don't get it."

"Up ahead. Look."

Laurel forces her head up and looks out the windshield. "God." She meant to say *oh my god,* but the stench in the car rips all the air out of her lungs. They're traveling up, the highway rising at a steep slant as if they're moving up the lengthy curve of a bridge, as if the bridge is moving away from the land and shooting up toward the purpling edges of coming night. The trees are gone, and so is everything else—no familiar mountain range jutting up from the distant peninsula or setting sun, and if there are cables and iron arches holding up the bridge, they are invisible against the cavernous bowl of the sky. Far ahead of them and moving closer, Laurel makes out an oily, shimmering movement, an oval-shaped darkness that seems to be eating away at the end of the bridge. She wants to say *what the fuck is that,* but all that comes out is a soft, breathy *fuuuuu.*

Mrs. Gibson is whispering, *sleep, sleep,* the words hot and wet against Laurel's neck. Laurel contorts her body as much as she can, recoiling from the woman's heat and touch. Maybe if there's still enough room, she can slide over into the back seat, and then out through the side door—as she tries to twist herself around, Laurel freezes. Mrs. Gibson is sitting with her hands in her lap, ankles crossed as if she's sitting in a church pew, waiting to drop four quarters into the collection plate. But her face is anything but calm and serene. Laurel has never seen such a look of determination, concentration, as if she's preparing for whatever they're rapidly approaching. Her hands rest in her lap.

"Oh my god—" Cold fear momentarily breaks through all the languid paralysis, and Laurel lurches into Mrs. Gibson, grabbing at the steering wheel. It's rigid and unmoving beneath her weak grasp. Underneath the dashboard, her feet thrash around the pedals, trying to find the break.

There's so little room—"Pull up your legs, if I can't steer the car, we're going to crash!"

"The car is being steered." Her voice is barely a whisper. "Keep still. Less painful."

"No, it is fucking *not*," she gasps into Mrs. Gibson's face. "What are you doing, what is happening?!"

"Rough crossing," the older woman replies, her lips barely moving. "You'll survive. You just need to make it through the bridge."

"What are you talking about!" Laurel shrieks. Overhead, the car roof buckles down in a screech of metal, and spiderweb cracks instantly radiate throughout the windshield. "We're not anywhere near the fucking water!"

"Look."

Laurel stares out the remains of the windshield, little slivers of cold wind threading through the cracks and slicing at her face. That musky animal scent, the dank smell of unwashed skin and genitals, thick overripe secretions bursting from swollen scent glands: it's coming from her. It's her.

Outside, the highway is flat against the horizon, growing smaller and smaller as it disappears into the pulsing, gobbling black dot. It's not perspective, Laurel realizes, as her body begins to violently shake. The highway, the car, the skies: they're all growing smaller, slipping into some hole or mouth or orifice so infinitesimal that it can barely be seen.

The entire front of the car smashes inward, as if a titan's invisible hands clapped and crushed a bug. A high-pitched scream fills the interior space: she knows it's coming from her, but it's not *of* her, the scream is its own creation, coiling out of her mouth like a frightened snake. The steering wheel has pushed forward into Mrs. Gibson's chest, she never had a chance to let out more than a wet muffled grunt before her chest crunched inward, and the car is still racing down the highway, no longer being steered but pulled. Laurel feels and hears the roaring engine, the wheels spinning against the pavement, there are no words for this pain, no words only bright images that explode like song from every part of her body that is now a mouth, and there is—

There is the car with all of its hard and sharp metal pieces and the dark engine collapsing into itself like a dying sun and there are human bones and all the beautiful strands of nerves and bones like liquid moving around the hot strips of car and their faces split open like decaying flowers and legs and arms rip away, replaced by strips of tires, pistons, shards of polished steel smashing their way up torsos and through hearts, and everything is growing smaller again. There are strands of blue electricity that crackle and pulse as they slide through and around the grinding mass of metal and flesh—the only sentient remains of two passengers traveling a cosmic route they could never have survived in their original form. There is liquid darkness, the elastic liquidity of pulverized organic matter as it passes through the hole, the liquid of the metals as it mingles with bones pulled into strands as long as epochs, rivers of engine oil and shit and blood and the faint chemical scent of paper trees and now it is a Planck length-wide being stretching across the arc of the universe, an infinitesimal ferry sailing through currents of time and pockets of antediluvian life with its two miniscule passengers, until it slows a billion years into an undiscovered future or past, pools out and down, sloughing off its cargo on a quiet gray island shore as it once again disappears into the unknown.

Little flecks of bone spiraling up from the goo, teeth pulling themselves out of paste and chromium drops, nerves and wires and cables spiraling back into a shape they remember only vaguely as a dream. Ravens shout in alarm from the trees as two shapes emerge and float away from the cauldron of chaos at the end of the bridge, a four-lane bridge that becomes a two-lane road disappearing into the somber stillness of a quiet coastal island, surrounded only by the gentle lapping of—

Waves crash down and in and recede, the sound flowing like broken glass over Laurel's body. With shaking fingers, she rubs her gummy eyes until they open. She stands on a beach that flows unbroken in both directions until it disappears with the curve of the land. The beach is wide and flat, a shore of smooth black and gray granite pebbles. Behind her, the edges of the beach are lined in long piles of smooth driftwood—entire tree trunks tangled with smaller branches, lengths of splintered timber, and the occasional pale ivory of broken skulls and bones. Beyond the driftwood rises an unbroken wall of evergreens.

She runs her hand over her face, arms, breasts, stomach. Under the reddish-brown layer of viscous gore, her body feels unsplit, unwounded. Laurel grabs at her hair. It hangs in wet chunks from her head, matted and sticky, but it's all there. She slicks her hand down her arm, trying to wipe off the semi-congealed blood. It sloughs off and plops to the wet rocks at her feet, but even as she raises her hand again, her skin ripples and contracts, sending another fresh layer to the surface. Laurel raises her fingers to her nose and inhales deeply. She knows this smell intimately, recognizes her own scents and the sticky texture of the chunky blood oozing from every pore in her skin. Overhead, a thousand pale moons shine weakly in the gray skies.

# NEW FOX SMELL

The sound of rocks crunch against each other: Laurel drops to a crouch and presses into the driftwood as a shape emerges from around the bend in the beach. Slender and tall, reddish-brown skin glistening under the light of the overcast skies. The shape pauses, looks furtively around, then stumbles forward. Laurel knows that face.

"P—Patricia?"

Two rows of glaringly white teeth emerge from the dry, brown-blooded sea of its face.

"It hurts the worst the first time. No way to avoid that, I'm sorry to say. Because you girls never obey me. You never listen to what I say."

Laurel whips her head up. Mrs. Gibson stands at the top of a small path winding through a break in the driftwood, her skin stained as dark as crushed blackberries, the pink lipstick obliterated from her mouth.

Laurel rises up from her crouch, fingers curling into fists. "Where are we? What happened to me?"

"We crossed the bridge, then took the ferry to Fox Island."

"This isn't—" Laurel turns and looks out across the gently lapping waters. Strange shapes move within the gray fog that coats the coastline, shapes as massive as buildings. Larger. A soft, thunderous rumble emanates from them, or some other unseen colossus, sending little quakes through the beach and up Laurel's body until she trembles in time with the vibrations. Further to the left, a shaft of dark light slashes through the fog and clouds like a sword, the low bass of a horn accompanying each rotation. There aren't any lighthouses along the Straits. There never have been.

"This isn't—where did you take me, where are we?"

Mrs. Gibson smiles. She wipes the blood away from her face: it stays off, the skin underneath remains pale and white. "I'd think the more pressing question would be, *what have I become*, or maybe, *where did I park the car*, but you can be forgiven for not quite understanding the situation."

A calm, cold numbness washes through Laurel, that she gradually realizes is a combination of white-hot rage and uncontrollable fear.

"What have I become?"

"You haven't *become* anything. You're simply in a place where you're more you than you could ever be. More girl than you were back home." Mrs. Gibson pulls a blood-soaked pack of cigarettes out of her jacket pocket and slides one out with her broken nails. "More animal. More alive."

"Take me back to the car, now."

"You better worry about your own engine, sweetheart," she says, turning away as she heads into the woods. "In fact, you and Patty had both better start running—they're headed right toward you!" she shouts back, coils of acrid smoke following her words. "They can smell you from a million miles away, and you no longer have that new car smell!" Laurel stares at the shadowed space between the trees where Mrs. Gibson used to be, then turns back to the beach.

"*What! The Fuck! Is going on!!*" Her ragged screams bounce back and forth across the waters. Immediately from within the looming gray bank of clouds, a roar claps back across the water, so unimaginably loud that all the driftwood along the shore clatters from the force of the sound. Wet warmth floods her crotch, trickles down her legs.

Patricia lopes past her in a quick animal gait. She's wiped her face clean, just like her mother. "You'll be the one, I know it. I told mom, this time I wanted someone who'd last the whole summer with me. Not a friend. Someone who'd hate me enough to survive."

"Survive what!?"

"Duh, the fox hunt, you dork!" she says with that familiar bright grin as she breaks into a run. Laurel watches as she grows smaller and smaller, disappearing around the curve of the island. She looks out at—the ocean? the Sound? Columns and mounds of dark flesh are beginning to take shape, slowly emerging from the storm and fog. Her feet are stepping back already, legs stumbling backwards up that little path, even though part of her wants so badly to see, to see. But the thought is fleeting and alien, that part of her brain is shutting down, and now Laurel's running, legs pumping like pistons through forest choked with green ferns and bramble, running until she's nothing more than a streak of fresh red on the ancient land, a pine and cunt-scented arrow pointing the way for the hounds and hunters to meet her at the end.

# A BETTER HATE

## PATRICK FREIVALD

CHRISTMAS LIGHTS TWINKLED throughout downtown, from power poles and street-shop windows, sparks of shimmering color outshining even the orange haze of sodium vapor bulbs polluting the quaint charm of Onageo Flats, New York. Wild packs of carolers sang on distant streets, voices quaking out harmonies in the unseasonable cold. Over the Red Coyote Bed and Breakfast, the lights flickered in the pre-solstice chill, and shadows played beneath them, turning once-jovial wreaths into ice-rimed specters.

Uncle George spat a gob of tobacco juice off the porch. Benny watched it skitter across snow glazed with a sheen of ice, frozen before it hit the ground.

"Manitou," George said.

Benny sighed through uncontrollable shudders his ridiculous puffy coat had no power to suppress. "No such thing as a manitou, Uncle George. High Hat's just some angry bigfoot knockoff displaced by the dam like the rest of us."

George spat again. "Not *a* manitou. Manitou. The way your ancestors meant it. This town's life-force is failing."

Benny's ancestors, as far as he knew, were more from Eastern Europe than the wilds of New York, but George always insisted their Algonquin blood overruled all that, "especially out here beyond the Western Door." Things like this were important to Uncle George, even a mile off the Reservation, so despite a waiting cup of hot chocolate with peppermint vodka and a wood stove set to blasting, Benny hunkered down further in his coat and stamped his feet in his too-thin boots and asked a question he didn't want answered.

"How's that?"

"When George Washington pushed the Mahican from the River, most fled north into Canada, but a few of us found another home among the Seneca people. Just a few of us. But we brought with us our manitou, our spirit, and even today it survives, even today it fights against the violence done to our bodies and our ways. Maybe the Onodowaga's manitou could have held this place, but the white man's manitou is weak, from stolen water. And it's failing."

The lights flickered again, and George raised a withered hand to gesture vaguely at them, as if they made some kind of point.

"That's just the wind, Uncle George." Another icy blast emphasized Benny's point. "The only vengeful spirit around here's in the shed. I think—"

"How can you think when you don't know? Kids today don't learn the history, don't learn the lore. All they do—"

Benny let the old man grumble-ramble a few minutes about the swampland drained to make the town and a dozen other things, then breathed a sigh of relief when Uncle George finally wheeled forward, the signal that he wanted to be pushed back inside, over the lip into the foyer, where the warm air scented with cloves and cinnamon hit them like a wall.

"—and now that it's come, you'll see it's nothing to laugh about."

"I wasn't laughing, Uncle George."

His mother—Uncle George's niece—bumped the door closed with her hip, then handed them both a cup of spiked hot chocolate as soon as they'd removed their coats.

"Leave the boy alone, George. It's Founder's Day!"

George glared at her with his one good eye over the steaming mug of cocoa. "All the more reason to take care, little girl. These times carry power, and it's not something to take lightly. This town is ripe for a harvest."

She snorted. "They're tourists, not grain."

"Much the same."

She scowled at him, he returned it, and Benny caught something unspoken he didn't understand, something he knew they wouldn't tolerate him asking about. George wheeled himself in front of the great room television and set about ignoring them in favor of *The Price is Right*.

Benny's mother's scowl turned into a smile as she turned to him. "Now finish your drink and check on the guests in room three. They didn't come down for dinner and maybe want some room service." She lowered her voice. "We could use the scratch, and that squash soup from Thursday isn't getting any fresher."

He bounded up the stairs and walked down the hall to what had once been his father's study, back when their home was a home and not a revenue-generating machine dependent upon tourists looking to carve out a slice of memories from a hunk of Americana, back when the town was just a dying coal-country town and not a hot-spot destination for those escaping "The City," be that Pittsburgh or New York or Philadelphia or even Cleveland.

Back when he had a father.

After three unanswered knocks, he tried the knob.

Icy air rushed from the open window, billowing the filmy, gossamer blinds that overlooked the Norman Rockwell downtown that had once been boggy marsh. Beneath the window, the Colemans lay entwined on the bed, mouths agape, eyes wide in the unending horror of death. Ice crusted their ravaged bodies, and purplish, ropy entrails lay scattered and spattered about the room. Bright red gore smeared the walls and soaked into the bedspread and mattress. Marlie's thigh and buttocks lay exposed, great hunks of muscle and fat torn from white bone. Andrew's left arm ended at the shoulder, a ragged, crimson mass of torn meat. His right foot lay next to the nightstand, shattered bone protruding where his toes should have been.

A pinprick pair of lights drew his eyes to the window. They grew larger, and larger still, to the size of quarters, bloodshot sclera and ice-blue irises ringed pupils so black they sucked in the universe. It blinked twice with sideways eyelids from deep under a knobby brow. The creature pulled back and, left-handed, set a giant stovepipe hat on its head. It grinned, and Christmas lights that should have come down a month ago twinkled in the bloody sheen on its serrated teeth.

Benny opened his mouth to scream, and the thing vanished from the window in a soaring leap onto the roof of the pastry shop next door.

He stumbled back, almost fell down the stairs, and when he reached the landing, wrapped his mother in an embrace. His gorge rose, and he swallowed the acrid bile into a stomach already churning.

"Abe is loose."

Her body went rigid. After a moment, she dug her nails into his arms, then released, took a deep breath.

"That stupid, pig-headed bastard," she said in his ear.

"We need to—"

"Son, let me worry about George. You know where it's going."

He sighed, deep and long, and tried not to let the fear creep into his voice.

"I'll get the gun."

Marcy put her hand on her uncle's shoulder. He reached up and squeezed it, his papery skin hot with fever.

"You let it free."

He wheezed by way of reply, anemic and weak.

"Why?"

George cleared his throat. "They took our land, killed our people, drove us—"

"Why *now*? We agreed Benny would be twenty. I had another year to train him."

"He's a man. And I couldn't bear one more Founding Day ceremony. Might not live to the next, and what then?"

"He's a *boy*, who knows too little of the old ways."

"And whose fault is that?"

"As much yours as mine. And his father's. And your brother's."

He grunted, as close as he ever came to a concession.

"I had another year."

"And now you do not."

"You unleashed a *demon*. Again, George."

George grunted. "High Hat is a demon, yes, but a *New World* demon, driven mad by the dam at Kinzua and the flooding of Cornplanter's grave. A New World wendigo needs a New World man to bring it to heel. The boy is up to it."

Despite herself, she snarled. "Tonight is the festival at the gazebo, you old fool. It's going to kill them all."

He chuckled. "All? No. Just enough. And that's why it had to be tonight. Hundreds gathered in their coats and mittens to see the town hall light up, chanting their prayers to their dead god in gratitude for stolen land and drowned magic. And when that building lies in ashes among their bodies, your boy will be a hero."

"You may have killed him."

After a long slurp of cocoa, George licked his lips.

"Maybe. But we all die, Marcy. And if you're right, then this . . . this isn't a mistake I'll live through." He held up his empty cup. "Be a dear and get me another?"

Benny caught the first footprint in the dirty snowbank next to Caruso's Café, a bloody smear over dingy white, and another bloody smear eight feet up on the streetlight pole. He already knew Red wouldn't track High Hat—dogs are smarter than humans on that score—but he had a good guess where the demon was headed.

He tried to ignore the tourists and erstwhile skiers frosting their lungs in the bitter cold, their wide eyes and shocked gasps at the shotgun. In thick gloves and a thicker coat, he had nowhere to hide it, no way to even make it less obvious. At least he held it halfway up the barrel, as unthreatening as possible a way to lug a gun down Main Street. Shivering in the bitter cold, a part of him burned with satisfaction at the ruination of their rituals—the leafers and the skiiers and Christmas crowd were bad enough to the townies even as they ate at their restaurants and shopped at their stores, but nothing beat the Founders Day rush for sheer bumbling stupidity, rushing to a nowhere town to celebrate its great whitening. The local stores, on and off-Reservation, even sold dreamcatchers and little carved totem poles in blue and white to Live Laugh Lovers too dumb to tell a Seneca from a Chippewa from a Tlingit. Or a Chinese sweat shop.

But none of the tourists ran, as they should have. A ten-foot giant with an Abe Lincoln hat should have scared the shit out of everyone, but they didn't run, no, they only gaped at *him*, the brown-skinned local with the shotgun. For a giant, High Hat had a way of not being seen. A manitou, or whatever the Seneca would call it; a spell.

Headlights rounded the corner behind him, washing the street with a sparkling glaze, a winter fairytale turned donut. The flicker of blue and red drew a groan from his throat quickly overwhelmed by the sharp blip from what had to be a police cruiser.

"Whoa, there, mister, where you going with that thing?"

Benny stretched his arm out, keeping the gun as harmless as possible without dropping it, and turned around. Even the police car had a blue and white bow on the hood. The spotlight blinded him, blasting even the headlights into so much after-image, and he squinted against the onslaught in a vain attempt to see.

"Hey," one of them said. "It's Marcy's boy." Then, louder, "What are you doing, Benny?"

*Tracking a giant cannibal my great uncle kept locked in the shed out back, of course.*

"Doing, Officer?"

"You can't bring a long arm to the festival, you know that, right?"

"I'm not going—" Only, *shit. That's exactly where I'm going.* "I'm just going . . . hunting."

"At night? This isn't the Reservation. Why don't you put the gun down and we can have a little talk."

"I'm kind of in a hurry." *And I've never even lived on the Reservation, you racist prick.*

He couldn't see it, but the unmistakable sound of a hocked loogie indicated the deputy's opinion of that statement.

"Not anymore. Put the gun derukkk—!"

The choking noise turned into a panting, keening wail. Gunshots rang out, a pistol maybe, six, seven shots.

"Jesus! Jed!"

Benny stumbled back, spun around the corner of the building and squeezed his eyes shut. Sparks of color danced around a giant blue after-image behind his eyelids.

The man's screaming cut off with a gurgle. Things snapped, like a boot on dry kindling, followed by a sloppy wet splash like spilled chili, then lip-smacking chewing noises.

Now people screamed. A lot of them.

He choked up the gun, got his fat, gloved finger on the trigger and the stock against his shoulder, opened his eyes to a squint and rounded the corner.

High Hat stood in front of the car, a cop hoisted one-handed above his head, face buried in his abdomen, slurping. The body shuddered and tried to kick, mouth wide and gaping, eyes wider still in uncomprehending panic. The other officer lay on the ground underneath High Hat's boot, neck spurting steaming blood across the pavement, turning the dirty snow cover black under the sodium glare.

Benny pointed the gun center-of-mass and pulled the trigger.

The blast deafened him, the flash another spot in his already-compromised vision.

High Hat's roar combined the worst aspects of a barking deer and a yowling mountain lion, a hundred times louder. Streetlights burst in a series of pops, and the blue-and-white strings of lights adorning the poles flared too bright to a burnt orange, then went out altogether.

Blinking, holding his breath, Benny strained to see with the police car's lights in his eyes. Nothing stood there—no hat, no glistening eyes, no serrated teeth.

He took a step, listened.

Another step, sweat freezing to his exposed forehead.

Nothing shuffled, nothing growled or roared or even breathed.

Another step. Both cops lay on the ground, literally in pieces, butchered meat strewn about the empty street. He dared suck in a trickle of frigid air that squeezed his lungs and hurt his lips. No odor rose from the dead officers, the cold robbing them even of the stink of death.

*Where'd you go, you poor fucker?*

Another step.

Finally behind the headlights, he picked up a pistol, checked the magazine—six rounds, to compliment the four left in his shotgun.

The lights had died several blocks in every direction, plunging the idyllic downtown into blackness under a gray-washed, cloudy sky. In that blackness, a twenty-foot flailing tube-man slowly deflated in front of the hardware store, but nothing else moved, nothing he could hear, nothing he could see.

"Abe? You out there, buddy?"

If High Hat heard, it didn't reply.

But in the distance, voices rose over a crackling speaker, singing the town's official hymn. "Herein Herein We Make Our Blessed Home" called townspeople and tourists alike to the gazebo for the annual lighting of the town hall.

Marcy brought him another cup, this one with a double-shot.

"Why the gazebo, Uncle? And why Founder's Day?"

George took a sip, then another.

"Well, why do you think I caught him there? Why did they center the town there, to hold their ceremonies and hang their criminals on that particular ground? What is it about that place?"

"I don't know. It just—you tell me."

"When they built the dam and flooded the Reservation, the Army Corps of Engineers condemned a half-dozen towns on either side of the border. The Onodowaga rebuilt in other sites where they could, but here? This is the killer. The white men drained the upland marsh, irrigated it right into the growing reservoir. All the birds and beavers and fish had nowhere to go. And neither did it. But unlike the *kìgònz* and *mikinàk*, the fish and the turtles, it couldn't just die and make way. So it stayed."

"It—that thing—*lived* there?"

"It doesn't live at all, not like you and me. Maybe it did, once, and maybe it didn't. I'm thinking it didn't."

"And why's that?"

"When I caught it, there wasn't much nothing there. No real spirit inside, not even a spark of manitou, nothing but emptiness, despair, and rage. A shell full of hate. Powerful, but it isn't hard to bind a thing like that."

"No?"

"No."

"Then how do you do it?"

"You give it something to hate *more*."

Brent Gallo waved and put on his best shit-eating grin, hoping his eyes carried what the crowd couldn't see behind the scarf. Three fingers of scotch hadn't touched the bitter cold, and three more felt wholly inadequate but sent his stomach into a queasy churn that threatened to explode out his ass at any moment.

Shitting himself in front of a couple hundred constituents and tourists held about as much appeal as dying of hypothermia for a fucking lighting ceremony. Three stories tall and bedecked with the finest livery these backwater rubes could afford, the wood and brick building looked a hell of a lot nicer than any of the homes or other buildings, and the roof shingles could likely beat most of those residents in a game of wits. At least the tourists had a little class. And the right habits, some of them.

It might have grown from a shit-hole swamp into a shimmering shit-hole tourist trap, but Onegeo Falls sat six hundred yards from the anything-goes Pennsylvania border and two miles from the fuck-it-bribe-me Reservation, which made it the perfect node for the movement of certain goods. Fireworks, mostly—the yeehaw rednecks in New York couldn't get the good stuff legally and paid out the nose for it—but also tax-free cigarettes, booze, and the occasional crate of firearms or brick of fentanyl-laced yay.

It almost made leaving Jersey City to rule this little plot of heaven worth it. At least for a while.

"Mr. Mayor?"

Speaking of yeehaw rednecks, Brent turned to his chief of staff, literally his only employee, the corn-fed and husky Denise Heron, built like a Saint Bernard and twice as smart, her teeth chattering in the frigid breeze. Oh, how he wanted to slap the "I Love NY" hat off her piggish head.

"What?"

"Th-th-there seems to be a problem."

He kept waving, thankful that the scarf hid his scowl.

"And that is?"

"Earl Buck—you know, at the, at the dam?—he's r-reporting a surge. It's pretty bad, and he's got to shhhhut down a g-generator or two to check it out." She rubbed her arms through her coat. "Jesus, it's cold."

"What are you saying to me?"

"He's going to turn off the t-town."

"He's going to—right *now*!? Is he *insane*?"

"Sir, it's pretty—"

"You tell him that when I flip this switch, if that fucking hall doesn't light up like a goddamned Christmas Tree, I'm going to shove the whole goddamned thing up his ass sideways, you understand me?"

"Yes, s-sir. But he's—"

"*TELL HIM!*"

Behind her, a pillar rose out of the well-trampled, snowy grass, too tall to have been there in the first place. Perhaps a foot in diameter, jet black and made of some kind of leather or hide, it carried wriggling shadows with it. At first he wasn't sure what he was seeing, but when the brim materialized, the image resolved into a stovepipe hat, well-weathered, fit for a giant Abraham Lincoln.

Coming right out of the ground.

White gloves followed, dirt sloughing off them without revealing the slightest stain, the tips removed to accommodate great curved claws like a cat's, only larger than any cat he'd ever seen.

He blinked. Shook his head. Blinked again.

It didn't help.

Denise shrieked as the claws dug into her thighs. The town went black.

Hot liquid splashed across his face as Denise's scream cut off. It tasted of raw meat and sick-up, like his mother's fazool minus the tomatoes left too long in the fridge, and stuck to the felt of his gloves as he pulled his fingertips from his lips.

"Denise?"

Hot, fetid breath washed across his face, and he gagged.

"Denise?"

In the darkness something twinkled, like a pair of flashlights with dying batteries.

*Eyes.*

"Denise?"

He reached out a gloved hand, and something took it.

Benny screeched to a halt in front of the town square, throwing him against the steering wheel as the squad car stopped way better than anything he'd driven. The lights died—all of them. Only his headlights lit the crowd, a sea of silhouettes under a black tree. As he got out, someone screamed—no, shrieked, an almost inhuman wail of agony. One by one a hundred pinpricks lit the square, phones sparkling through the crowd with bright white LEDs.

"Oh, my God!" a man yelled.

Lights turned, and drowned in a thirteen-foot shadow, ravenous darkness in a ridiculous hat. High Hat's body swallowed the light, leaving visible only a pair of white gloves, glittering eyes, and teeth stained red with glistening fluid. Mayor Gallo's head stared out from its gaping maw, just long enough to burst in a red gush as those massive teeth snapped shut.

The giant exploded into the crowd in a spray of disembodied limbs, severed heads and crushed torsos. They broke, a screaming panic of bobbing phone lights, pushing Benny back against the car. He scrambled onto the hood to escape the press of bodies and choked up the gun.

"Abe! Hey Abe! I'm over here!"

High Hat turned at his nickname, the one Benny had used for as long as he could remember, the one he used when he delivered meals to the shed, the one he'd used when, at nine years old, he'd freed the creature in a fit of pity, only to have it kill his mutt Barney and two passers-by on its way to the gazebo. The name he'd used when he'd cried apologies to it, begging forgiveness after Uncle George closed the manacles back onto its wrists and ankles.

High Hat cocked its head, squinted its sideways eyes against the headlights, still chewing on a wayward arm through cloudy gusts of hot breath. If his earlier shotgun blast had hurt it, Benny saw no sign of it.

*Closer.*

"C'mon, Buddy. You don't have to hurt these people. I'm not going to take you back. Can we—can we just leave? Go somewhere . . . nicer?"

It took a step toward him, turned to look at the gazebo, then back to him.

Benny hopped off the car, lowered the shotgun.

"Just you and me. We can find a nice marsh for you to live in, with lots of ducks and turtles and raccoons, far away from . . . all this."

It took a step toward him, and he answered with one of his own.

Then another.

"That's it, Abe. I'm not gonna hurt ya."

High Hat's eyes narrowed to vertical slits, and a deep rumble growled forth from its throat.

"No, really, I'm not." Benny realized that he meant it.

He crouched, set the shotgun on the ground, and stood with his hands raised.

"There's a huge swamp out east, near Syracuse. It's called Montezuma."

He took a step, and High Hat matched it. His voice shook, but he kept talking, kept walking.

"No hunters—they're not allowed. All the deer you can eat. Deer and bear and coyotes, sometimes maybe a jogger, but you got to avoid the DEC guys. Take any of them and you won't be able to hide."

They'd closed the distance to just a few steps.

"It'll be nice. I promise."

He opened his arms wide. High Hat leaned in, snorting and sniffling, charnel-house breath filling Benny's nostrils with the cloying smell of rotten meat and shit and acrid bile. The creature's serrated teeth brushed against his neck. Hot piss streaked down his legs, soaking his boxers and jeans and trickling into his boots.

Even so, he reached out, put his hand on the thing's chest—thick, wiry, wolflike hair somehow wispy and ephemeral, like spider silk that broke at his touch and reformed behind it.

"What do you say, Abe? All you got to do is come back home."

Its roar deafened him, hot spittle and worse things spattering across his face stung his eyes and set his lungs on fire. It reached down and clawed hands grabbed his wrists, wrenching them away from the pistol in his belt. It roared again, his head halfway in its mouth, a thick red tongue split like a serpent's flicking up and down his cheeks.

Pinpricks jabbed his throat and the back of his head.

"No, please, no. Abe, please!"

His breath left him as a hundred serrated knives sank into his neck and skull, each fraction of an inch an unending agony. He flailed and kicked as his flesh separated and blood flowed into the monster's mouth, but his feet had left the ground, and Benny had no purchase, no hope of overpowering the thing.

*I'm sorry, Mom. I've failed you.* He sent his dying thoughts to Bi-bon, the North Wind that brought the winter, that it might carry them to his mother.

High Hat chuckled, a deep, unwholesome rumble that shredded his flesh further. Blood welled in his throat, and he squeezed his eyes shut against the pain.

"*Widjigo*!" His mother's voice rang out in the silence of the night. She spoke rapid-fire in the lost language of the Mahicans, the language she and Uncle George had tried to teach him, that he'd been too impatient to learn.

It opened its mouth and turned its head without letting him go. Blood gushed from his wounds into his coat, hot and sticky yet so, so cold.

She stood on the gazebo, one hand on Uncle George's shoulder. Scraps of cloth bound the old man's arms to the wheelchair, and another formed a gag. He stared at High Hat, his eyes wide with terror, a stark contrast to the otherworldly calm he'd carried with him for so many years.

She spoke again, and in his mind's ear Benny understood her.

"My son offered you a fair bargain, and I seal it with this: my uncle, George Runs-With-the-Hare, who bound you these many decades, who kept you from your home, from your vengeance, from your rightful place alongside the *Pagwadjininì* from which you were born. I know you hate him, as you hate these savages who stole your land, drowned the land of your people, and drained the water that nourished and fed you and yours. With this hate, *widjigo*, I bind you to honor my son's bargain. With this hate, *widjigo*, I bind you to leave this land for another. With this hate, *widjigo*, I bind you to live out your days doing no harm to the Mahican, no harm to the Onodowaga."

Benny fell to his hands and knees as High Hat dropped him.

He struggled to right himself, struggled to keep his vision straight, cold-thickened blood oozing down his neck into his clothes. As the beast stalked toward his mother, Benny pulled the gun from his belt. Aiming through a haze of blood and pain, only his mother's upraised hand stopped him from pulling the trigger.

When the creature reached Uncle George, the streetlights flickered to life. As sickly orange merged with twinkling sparks of color, High Hat faded into shadow, and then into nothing. The speakers stuttered to life, "Herein Herein We Make Our Blessed Home" blaring out across the blood-soaked commons, calling out to trampled and slaughtered bodies, to broken tourists wailing for their loved ones.

Benny leaned back against the car, and lifted his hands to his neck. Thick, gelatinous blood oozed but did not gush from his wounds.

His mother looked down at him and smiled. "That's going to leave quite a scar. I'm proud of you, Son."

Uncle George said nothing, but blinked once with odd, sideways eyelids.

"Come on, let's get you to the car. We've a promise to keep."

They pulled onto the Thruway shoulder at three-fifteen a.m., well after the bars closed, well before the morning rush. The gibbous moon and fading stars cast the area into a black-and-white mosaic, tinged only at the edges by the hazy orange glows from Seneca Falls, Auburn, and far-off Syracuse. No frogs or insects sounded in the February chill, but deer barked and scattered as they heaved and hauled Uncle George's catatonic body over the chain-link fence and into the Montezuma Wildlife Refuge. Benny did most of the carrying, though his mother helped with the occasional drag across the hard-packed, frozen swamp.

Once out of sight of the road, they tucked him into the hollow of a fallen tree. Benny's mother leaned in and whispered words he couldn't hear, and shadows claimed his uncle's body, which became a swimming darkness with a pair of bloodshot eyes. Those eyes and a grin of serrated teeth faded into nothing, and for a moment the trees shivered.

"Bye, Abe." Benny patted the log, and stood, and waited, his head a war of melancholy and relief.

After a while, he scratched at the scabs on his neck, and his mother put her hand on his shoulder.

"Are you finished?"

He chuckled. "I was waiting for you."

She smiled. "Then let's get out of here. The Schneiders want their breakfast at seven."

# ABOUT THE AUTHORS

**S.C. Mendes** is the co-host of Horror Business—a podcast dedicated to helping authors make a career of their writing—and the producer of Don't Fall Asleep. Along with narrator Spencer Dillehay, Don't Fall Asleep delivers free audio recordings of scary stories from around the world and is available on Amazon, Google, Apple Spotify, YouTube, and more.

As an author and editor, Mendes has been publishing dark fiction since 2009 and is co-owner of Blood Bound Books. He is currently working on the third book in *The City* series, and his collaborations with Nikki Noir can be found in her Petite Mort series.

**Mark C. Scioneaux** is a Bram Stoker Award® nominated editor and author.

He is the author of numerous short stories appearing in various anthologies; most recently "A Very Trying Time" in *Distorted Mirrors,* published by Gyldendal of Denmark. He is the author of *Family Dinner, Slipway Grey, The Director's Cut,* and *Dead on The Bayou.* He is also author of the "Splattire Series" with books that include *Cannibal Fat Camp, Die, You Zombie Crackers!,* and *America's Next Dead Model.*

*Horror For Good: A Charitable Anthology* is an award-nominated anthology for charity he edited. *Blood Bank* is his latest anthology, co-edited and published by Blood Bound Books.

He is a graduate of Louisiana State University and currently resides in Baton Rouge, Louisiana with his wife, Kristin

**Joseph Spagnola** was born in Chicago, Illinois and has a bachelor's in management from University of Phoenix. As an insurance sales agent for the last decade, he knows what scares you. His obsession with reading started later in life which fueled his passion for encouraging others to become literate at an early age. He co-founded Blood Bound Books in 2009.

**Jo Kaplan** is a Los Angeles based writer also known as Joanna Parypinski. She is the author of the novels *It Will Just Be Us* and *When the Night Bells Ring*. Her short fiction has appeared in Fireside Quarterly, Black Static, Nightmare Magazine, Vastarien, *Haunted Nights* edited by Ellen Datlow and Lisa Morton, and Bram Stoker Award nominated anthology *Miscreations: Gods, Monstrosities & Other Horrors*. She teaches English and creative writing at Glendale Community College.

**Rena Mason** is the three-time Bram Stoker Award® winning horror and dark speculative fiction author of *The Evolutionist* and "The Devil's Throat" as well as a 2014 Stage 32 /The Blood List Search for New Blood Screenwriting Contest Quarter-Finalist. She recently co-edited *Other Terrors: An Inclusive Anthology* for the HWA Presents series out July 19, 2022 by Mariner Books.

She's a member of the Horror Writers Association, Mystery Writers of America, International Thriller Writers, The International Screenwriters' Association, and the Public Safety Writers Association.

An R.N. and avid scuba diver, she travels the world and incorporates the experiences into her stories. She currently resides in the Pacific Northwest.

For more information visit her website: www.RenaMason.Ink
or follow her at:
Facebook: rena.mason
Twitter: @RenaMason88
Stage 32: Rena Mason
Instagram: rena.mason

**Jeff Strand** is a five-time nominee (and zero-time winner, but c'mon, he lost to Stephen King TWICE!) of the Bram Stoker Award. He is a two-time nominee and one-time WINNER!!!! of the Splatterpunk Award.

His novels are usually classified as horror, but they're really all over the place, almost always with a great big dose of humor. He's written five young adult novels that all fall into the "really goofy comedy" category.

Several of his books are in development as motion pictures, and he's mostly not allowed to blab any details, which he finds MADDENING.

He lives in Chattanooga, Tennessee with his wife and one gigantic freaking cat.

**Neil Gaiman** is the #1 New York Times bestselling author of more than twenty books, including *Norse Mythology, Neverwhere*, and *The Graveyard Book*. Among his numerous literary awards are the Newbery and Carnegie medals, and the Hugo, Nebula, World Fantasy, and Will Eisner awards. He is a Professor in the Arts at Bard College.

Hailed by BOOKLIST as "one of the most clever and original talents in contemporary horror," **Kealan Patrick Burke** was born and raised in Ireland and emigrated to the United States a few weeks before 9/11. Since then, he has written five novels, among them the popular southern gothic slasher *Kin*, and over two hundred short stories and novellas, including *Peekers, Sour Candy* and *The House on Abigail Lane*, all of which have been optioned for film.

A five-time Bram Stoker Award-nominee, Burke won the award in 2005 for his coming-of-age novella *The Turtle Boy*, the first book in the acclaimed Timmy Quinn series.

As editor, he helmed the anthologies *Night Visions 12, Taverns of The Dead*, and *Quietly Now*, a tribute anthology to one of Burke's influences, the late Charles L. Grant.

Most recently, he adapted his work to comic book format for four volumes of John Carpenter's *Tales for a Halloween Night* series of anthologies and contributed a short story to Mike Mignola and Christopher Golden's *Hellboy: An Assortment of Horrors*. He is currently at work on a new novel, *Mr. Stitch*.

Kealan is represented by Merrilee Heifetz at Writers House.

He lives in an unhaunted house in Ohio with a Scooby Doo lookalike rescue pup named Red.

**Kristopher Triana** is the Splatterpunk Award-winning author of *Gone to See the River Man, Full Brutal, The Thirteenth Koyote, They All Died Screaming,* and many other terrifying books. His work has been published in multiple languages and has appeared in many anthologies and magazines, drawing praise from Rue Morgue Magazine, Cemetery Dance, Scream Magazine, and many more.

He lives in New England.
Kristophertriana.com
Twitter: Koyotekris
Facebook: Kristopher Triana
Instagram: Kristopher_Triana

**Jeremy Robert Johnson** is the author of *The Loop, Entropy in Bloom, In the River, All the Wrong Ideas,* and *Skullcrack City*. In 2008 he worked with The Mars Volta to tell the story behind their Grammy Winning album *The Bedlam in Goliath*. In 2010 he spoke about weirdness and metaphor as a survival tool at the Fractal 10 conference in Medellin, Colombia. In 2017 Jeremy's short story "When Susurrus Stirs" was adapted for film and won 14 awards including Best Short Film at the H.P. Lovecraft Film Festival and the Final Frame Grand Prize. Jeremy is at work on a host of new books. For more information: www.jeremyrobertjohnson.com.

**Mona Kabbani** is a horror fan, writer, and reviewer obsessed with psychology and the human condition. She emulates the conflict of the good versus the bad and all of the in between in her work while providing an entertainingly horrifying experience. She is a Lebanese immigrant living the American dream in New York City where much of her writing is inspired. You can follow her on Instagram @moralityinhorror for more and sign up to her mailing list on her website, www.moralityinhorror.com.

**Joseph Sale** is a prolific novelist, editor, and co-host of the Magical Writing podcast (along with S. C. Mendes). His first novel, *The Darkest Touch,* was published by Dark Hall Press in 2014. He has authored more than twenty books, including his *Black Gate* trilogy and his portal fantasy adventure *Dark Hilarity*. He grew up in the Lovecraftian seaside town of Bournemouth. His short work has appeared in anthologies such as Blood Bound Book's *Burnt Fur, Tales From The Shadow Booth* (edited by Dan Coxon), Storgy's *Exit Earth,* and many more alongside writers such as Neil Gaiman and Richard Thomas. If you love his work you can subscribe to his Patreon: https://www.patreon.com/themindflayer

**Max Booth III** is the editor of Ghoulish Books, the host/producer of the *Ghoulish* podcast, and the author of *Maggots Screaming!*. He wrote and produced the movie *We Need to Do Something* for IFC Midnight. Follow him on Twitter @GiveMeYourTeeth

**Lucy Leitner** is an advertising writer and award-winning journalist in Pittsburgh, PA.

Her transgressive fiction includes *Outrage: Level 10, Working Stiffs*, the novelette "Karen," and several shorter works that appear in anthologies and Godless original series.

She co-hosts HORROR BUSINESS with S.C. Mendes—a podcast dedicated to helping authors make a career of their writing. You can find her at LucyLeitner.com and @Lucy.Leitner on TikTok and Instagram.

**Jay Wilburn** is an author of horror and speculative fiction that lives in coastal South Carolina near Myrtle Beach. He is doing very well following a life-saving kidney transplant. He taught public school for sixteen years before becoming a full-time writer. His signature series is the *Dead Song Legend Dodecology* and for younger readers, *The Lake Scatter Wood Tales*. Follow his many musings @AmongTheZombies on Twitter, the Jay Wilburn author page on Facebook, and at JayWilburn.com. Jay Wilburn has a lot of original content on his Patreon page including a serial vampire novel and more. Patreon.com/JayWilburn Or catch him streaming live on Twitch. Twitch.tv/JayWilburn

**Livia Llewellyn** is a writer of dark fantasy, horror, and erotica, whose fiction has appeared in over 80 anthologies and magazines, including *The Best Horror of the Year, Year's Best Weird Fiction,* and *The Mammoth Book of Best New Erotica.* Her short fiction collections *Engines of Desire: Tales of Love & Other Horrors* (Lethe Press) and *Furnace* (Word Horde Press) were both nominated for the Shirley Jackson Award, and her short story "One of These Nights" won the 2020 Edgar Award for Best Short Story. You can find her online at liviallewellyn.com and on Twitter and Instagram.

**Patrick Freivald** is a four-time Bram Stoker Award® nominated author, a high school teacher (physics, robotics, American Sign Language), and a beekeeper specializing in hot pepper infused honey. He lives in Western New York with his beautiful wife, parrots, dogs, cats, chickens, and several million stinging insects. A member of the Horror Writers Association and the International Thriller Writers, he's always had a soft spot for slavering monsters of all kinds. The author of nine novels and dozens of short stories, from hyper-violent kickass thrillers and teen zombie melodramas to science fiction, horror and fantasy, you can find him at Patrick.Freivald.com, on Facebook, Instagram, Twitter, YouTube, and at www.FrogsPointHoney.com.

# ACKNOWLEDGMENTS

We'd like to thank the following for their special support in making Blood Bank a huge success!

Karen Lehrone, Nikolas P. Robinson, Dakota Dawe, Kelly Jones, Matt Miller, Nikki James, Sophie Allen-Etchart, Katie Herrick, Christian Vessell, William Jones, Wendy White, Johnny Spagnola, Karen Fierro, Nate Kolodziej, James Boyer, Richard Ciccarone, and of course, Christina Pfeiffer.

Made in the USA
Monee, IL
15 October 2024

67259869R10094